LIGHT OF HOPE

Light
of Hope

ROBERT VAUGHAN

A TOM DOHERTY ASSOCIATES BOOK
NEW YORK

LIGHT OF HOPE

Copyright © 2004 by Robert Vaughan

This book is printed on acid-free paper.

A Forge Book
Published by Tom Doherty Associates, LLC
175 Fifth Avenue
New York, NY 10010

www.tor.com

Forge® is a registered trademark of Tom Doherty Associates, LLC.

Library of Congress Cataloging-in-Publication Data

Vaughan, Robert.
    Light of hope / Robert Vaughan.—1st ed.
        p.   cm.
    "A Tom Doherty Associates book."
    ISBN 0-765-30947-5 (acid free paper)
    EAN 978-0-765-30947-1
    1. Widowers—Fiction. 2. Petroleum industry and trade—Fiction. 3. Women environmentalists—Fiction. 4. Single fathers—Fiction. 5. Women teachers—Fiction. 6. Alaska—Fiction. I. Title.

PS3572.A93L54 2004
813'.54—dc22

                                                                    2004050299

First Edition: November 2004

Printed in the United States of America

0   9   8   7   6   5   4   3   2   1

To my sons
Joe and Tom,
gifts from Alaska

LIGHT OF HOPE

~ *One* ~

Northern Alaska

The De Long Mountains towered over the snow-covered tundra of Alaska's Kukpuk River valley. Although barren of trees, the tundra was home to a wide variety of flora and fauna, as well as arctic wolves, foxes, brown and grizzly bears, ground squirrels and other small rodents. It was also home to caribou, and on this day in mid-November, a large, migratory herd was pawing at the snow in order to get to the vegetation below.

Suddenly the lead bull raised his head and began sniffing the wind. He sensed some sort of danger, but wasn't sure what it was, because he didn't see or smell anything. Still, something had disturbed him and, as the other caribou grazed contentedly, he continued to peruse the area, ever vigilant on behalf of those animals in his charge.

Then he heard it, an intrusive sound that was unnatural to him. He couldn't know it, of course, but his territory was being invaded by an unwelcome intruder, a ski-equipped airplane, letting down from above. The De Havilland Otter, quite large for a single-engine airplane, touched down, then slid for several feet on its skids until finally coming to a stop. The pilot gunned the engine and turned the plane around, then throttled back to idle so that the engine was barely ticking over.

From the back of the fuselage a door opened and several canvas bags were tossed out onto the snow. The packs were followed by four men and a woman. They were indistinguishable from one another because of the ruffed hoods, down parkas and pants, mittens, and mukluks all were wearing as protection against the below-zero temperature.

The leader of the group, Luke Koonook, walked up to the front of the plane and yelled up at the pilot.

"Pick us up in three days!"

"Three days. Will do!" the pilot replied.

He advanced the throttle and the five who had just deplaned turned their backs to the prop wash as the Otter started back down the snow-pack. It gathered speed quickly, lifted from the ground, then headed west. They watched for a moment longer as the engine sound diminished and the plane grew smaller.

Then, when it was gone, they were overwhelmed by the sound of silence.

"All right," Koonook said. "Let's get unpacked, then start after the caribou."

The lone woman of the group was Ellie Springer, a twenty-four-year-old blonde from Dallas, Texas. With green eyes, high cheekbones, and a lithe, lean body, she was very pretty, but presented herself in the unselfconscious way of someone who is unaware of her own attractiveness. Ellie was not only the only woman of the group, she was the only *nalokme,* as the Eskimos called the non-natives.

"Ellie, do you need any help getting unpacked?" Koonook asked.

"No. I'm fine," she answered.

A graduate of SMU with a B.S. in education, Ellie had taught school for two years in Dallas before applying for, and accepting, a position with the North Slope Borough School System. She now taught the fourth grade in Point Hope, Alaska.

As Ellie got her gear out of the canvas bag, she looked at the others. Luke Koonook was not only the leader of the hunting party, he was also the mayor of the village of Point Hope. He was the oldest of the group.

Ellie was the youngest, but Isaac Ahlook was only a few years older. The other two hunters, Mark Hale and Percy Tokomik, were first cousins.

Working quickly, they erected the tent that would be their shelter for the next three days. Then, with the tent erected and all their gear stowed, Luke picked up his rifle.

"Let's go get some meat."

The sky wasn't blue, but a washed-out white that almost perfectly matched the snow in color. The result was a blending of earth and sky that would have made it very difficult to establish the horizon had it not been for the mountain range.

The five hunters were walking abreast, taking their lead from Koonook. The temperature hovered around zero, and as they breathed, the vapor cloud hung in place glistening with tiny ice crystals.

Although this was an adventure, it was more than just an exciting escapade. In fact, it was a very necessary part of village life. The migratory caribou herd normally supplied the village with all the meat they would need. But when the herd moved too far inland for the hunters to get to them on foot, or by snowmobile, the village council chartered a plane for their five best hunters.

The plane had brought them nearly one hundred miles inland from Point Hope, and although it was noon, the sun was as high as it was going to get at this time of the year. It hung now like a great red ball, very low on the southern horizon.

Ellie was along for the hunt, because she had proven herself on previous hunting expeditions. Even before that, she had come to their notice the first summer she was in Point Hope when she won a shooting match, outshooting everyone in the village and half a dozen of the best shots from some of the nearby villages.

"When we reach the herd, Ellie will take the first shot," Koonook told the others.

This wasn't a "ladies first" gesture. He was giving Ellie the first shot as a matter of practicality. It was very important to get a caribou at the first encounter to establish the precedence of the hunt. Because of that, the best marksperson of the group was always selected to take the first shot. When Koonook chose Ellie, none of the others questioned the decision.

The villagers had been surprised at how well Ellie could shoot. They had no idea she learned her marksmanship from her father, who, for the last thirty years, had been the best marksman in the Dallas Police Department.

As they continued their trek across the tundra, Ellie recalled her father's chagrin when she told him she was going to teach school in Alaska.

"Why on earth would you want to go to such a place?" her father had asked.

"Think about it, Dad. I could continue to teach right here at Brentwood Elementary, two blocks from where I grew up, or I could go to Point Hope, Alaska, a place that most people can only read about. Just on the surface of it, which do you think sounds more exciting?"

"I thought you were trying to build a career," her father said. "I had no idea you were seeking a life of adventure."

"The two need not be mutually exclusive," Ellie replied. "Look at your own career."

The wind increased and the chill factor dropped to well below zero. Then, carried on the wind, they heard the faint sound of the caribou on the move.

"Listen! I hear them!" Ahlook said excitedly.

"Sshh," Koonook said, holding his mitten across his lips. "Quiet, that they do not hear us."

They moved ahead, even quieter than before. Then Koonook saw them. He held up his hand and pointed. The others nodded, indicating they had seen the herd as well.

The five hunters moved closer, ever closer to the herd. Once, a large bull raised his head and looked around warily, sniffing in the wind. Koonook pointed to him.

"He's the leader," Koonook said. "Look how the others continue to eat, unafraid. That's because they know he will warn them."

"He is beautiful," Ellie said.

"Yes, he is, but you must shoot him first. Without him to warn them, the others will not be so quick to run."

Ellie nodded, then raised the rifle to her shoulder.

For just a moment, she felt a twinge of regret over having to kill this magnificent creature. But she put that thought out of her mind and concentrated instead on the importance of this hunt to the village. The pack ice had already moved in and that meant there would be no more supply ships. Caribou, then, would be the principal source meat until the summer thaw.

Ellie took up a good sight picture of the caribou, aiming just behind the neck, approximately where she thought the animal's heart would be. She took a deep breath, let half of it out, then started increasing the pressure on the trigger.

She kept increasing the pressure gradually until the rifle roared and bucked back against her shoulder. Almost immediately after that, the bull caribou jumped slightly. He started forward a few steps, then stopped again. His front legs wobbled, then folded as he collapsed, nose-down into the snow.

"You got him!" Koonook said.

"Yes." Ellie was smiling broadly at her success.

"Shoot!" Koonook called to the others, and everyone raised their rifle. With the subsequent volley of shots the herd bolted, leaving behind, in addition to their fallen leader, three more animals on the ground.

On the morning of the day the plane was to return for them, the weather began to turn. The wind that was but a brisk breeze yesterday developed now into a full-blown gale. And on the heels of the wind was a very heavy snowstorm.

"This is not good," Tokomik said. "The plane will not be able to come for us until this storm is over."

Even as Tokomik was talking, the wind speed continued to increase and was now howling across the tundra at fifty miles per hour, blowing snow before it. It was impossible to separate the currently falling snow from snow that was whipped up from the surface. No matter which it was, it created a whiteout condition.

"We'd better tie ourselves together," Koonook said.

At Koonook's suggestion, Ellie and the four men tied themselves together with long strips of rawhide. She didn't question this because, even though all five were standing together, the intensity of the storm was such that she could see only the person nearest her.

"Okay, now that we can't get separated from each other, we'd better get busy and secure the tent."

Again, nobody questioned Koonook's suggestion. He was universally accepted as the leader of the group and, under such conditions, everyone knew that it was very important to give the leader unquestioned support.

Grabbing their small, collapsible shovels, they began to work, piling snow up around the base of the tent walls, then higher, and higher still until a wall of snow completely surrounded the tent. With the tent now secure, and the wind-borne snow still blowing painfully against them, the little band of hunters moved inside. There Ellie discovered, to her pleasant surprise, that the wall of snow not only protected the tent, it also provided additional insulation. As a result, the little Coleman camp stove managed to keep the inside of the tent comfortably warm.

Koonook settled down in one corner of the tent. "Now we wait," he said.

Their original hunting expedition was planned for three days, and they had brought enough provisions to last that long. But it was standard procedure for all hunters and fishermen to take an extra three days of emergency rations with them, for just such cases as this, so they were prepared to wait out the weather.

Everyone brought their own choice of survival food. For the four Eskimos, it was jerky and tins of sardines. For Ellie, it was a type of trail mix consisting of dried fruit, nuts, and M&Ms.

On the first three nights of the hunting expedition sleep had come quickly, partially because of exhaustion, but also because of the elation over their success. What conversation there was centered on the hunt, replaying the events of the day, or deciding where the herd would be the next day.

Tonight, which was the first night beyond their scheduled return, conversation was sporadic at best, finally stopping altogether. Sleep didn't come as quickly for Ellie as it did for the others, perhaps because they were less worried than she was. They had all been through something like this before, for nearly every Eskimo in the village had at least one survival adventure to tell. This experience would just add to their repertoire of stories.

Ellie was sure she was the last one awake, and she lay there in the darkness, listening to the snores and heavy breathing of the others. She didn't believe she had ever been in such darkness. Sliding her hand out from under her sleeping bag, she held it in front of her face.

She giggled quietly. It's true, she thought. It really can be so dark that you can't see your hand in front of your face.

Ellie thought of Maggie, and hoped that the Keatings would take care of her tonight.

Maggie was her wire-haired Jack Russell terrier, and though dogs were very common in Point Hope, most of them were working dogs such as huskies or malamutes. Maggie's only purpose was to keep Ellie company, and that she did very well.

Sam and Judy Keating shared a faculty duplex with her, near the Tikigaq School, as the Point Hope school where Ellie taught was called. Sunshine Komack, a teachers' assistant, was covering for her in the classroom while she was away on the hunt. And because Sam was also the principal, he was Ellie's boss. The Keatings were as crazy about Maggie as Ellie was, so she was sure that Maggie was being well taken care of. But Ellie knew, too, that Maggie would be wondering where she was.

Finally, content that Maggie was okay and that she was in good hands, Ellie managed to drift off to sleep.

*   *   *

Judy Keating stood in the living room, staring out the window.

"It's clear here now, but what if it decides to clear up where they are, and starts snowing here? The pilot still wouldn't be able to pick them up," she said.

Sam was sitting on the sofa, playing tug-of-war with the little chew toy that Maggie had brought him.

"Stop worrying about her, Judy," Sam said. "She's with Luke Koonook. If I had to be stranded out on the tundra with somebody, I can't think of anyone I would rather be stranded with."

"At least I know she has her survival kit with her," Judy said. "We talked about it before she left."

Sam laughed, as much to bolster his own spirits as Judy's. "Luke Koonook *is* a survival kit."

"But what if the storm lasts for several days?"

"Maggie will be all right with us," Sam said. "Won't you, Maggie?"

Maggie twisted her head slightly and looked at Sam, focusing hard to understand him.

"And, if I know Ellie, she's probably more worried about Maggie than she is about herself," Sam added.

The storm continued unabated for three days. During that time, the five entertained each other with stories from their past. But as the four men had grown up together in the same small village, they knew all of each other's stories, in fact were participants in them. When one of the men started a story, the others could pick it up in the middle and continue on. Despite that, Ellie found the stories fascinating and listened intently to each one. They were little windows onto this new and different culture she had entered.

"Soon it will be Christmas," Mark Hale said. "I wonder who will be Santa Claus this year?"

"The council hasn't chosen yet, have they?" one of the others asked.

"I think it will be Gus Kowanna," Koonook said.

"Not Gus. He's too mean to be Santa Claus. He will scare the children," Ahlook said.

"Is David looking forward to Christmas? Or is he still too young?" Ellie asked.

Ellie was talking about Ahlook's two-year-old son.

"He's too young to know anything about it, but he'll enjoy the celebration when it starts," Ahlook said.

"I think it's wonderful the way the entire village comes together for Christmas," Ellie said. "It's the best thing about living up here."

"Let's teach Miss Springer some of the traditional songs," Koonook suggested.

"Percy Tokomik can sing the best. Let him do it," Hale said.

Tokomik agreed, and began to sing for Ellie's benefit. But as the songs were in Eskimo dialect, they were practically impossible for her to learn.

"We've heard all of our stories," Koonook said to Ellie. "But you have been to places we have never seen. Tell us something of those places."

Ellie began, and for the next hour or so, the men were fascinated by her stories of growing up in a large city. She had seen, admittedly from a crowd, many famous people that the four men had only heard of, including Presidents George H. W. Bush, Bill Clinton, and George W. Bush. She had actually met and spoken with Laura Bush when she was First Lady of Texas.

When the five hunters stepped outside on the morning of the sixth day, they emerged into a pristine blanket of snow that covered everything in sight. The tent was now so completely covered by snow that it looked much more like the popular conception of an igloo than a canvas tent.

From no more than fifty feet away, their campsite couldn't be seen, having blended into the waves, ridges, and snowdrifts of the tundra. There were no footprints, no signs of their presence. There was nothing to distinguish their encampment from the hundreds of square miles it encompassed.

"I think the plane will come today," Koonook said. "So we must make a signal for him."

All five hunters carried out large, square, bright red banners. They laid down their banners in the form of a cross so that to any aviator, the bright red cross would be visible against the white snow from miles away.

Just after noon they heard the sound of an airplane engine.

"Is it coming for us?" Koonook asked, almost disinterestedly.

Mark Hale stared off into the distance. "Yes," he said. "It's the same Otter that brought us in."

"Only one?" Ahlook said.

"Yes, only one. Why? How many do you think we need?" Mark replied.

"Two," Ahlook replied. "One for us and the caribou we killed, and another one just for the caribou Ellie killed."

Ahlook was teasing, but it was a respectful recognition of the contribution Ellie had made to the success of this hunting trip.

~ *Two* ~

The women employees of Pangaea Oil had selected Galen Scobey as their most eligible bachelor.

"Why, he could pass as Matt Damon," one of the women said gushingly.

"No, Matt is too 'pretty.' Galen looks more like Damon's friend, Ben Affleck."

"Yes, that's who I was trying to think of," the first woman said.

Though he wasn't married, Galen would be more properly described as a widower than a bachelor. His wife, Julia, had died seven years ago, leaving him with a two-year-old boy.

Nelson—or Nels, as he was called—was now nine, and this evening he was riding in the car with his father as Galen had to go into the office. After he took care of some business in the office, they planned to go out for "Mexican." This was a concession to Nels, because it was his favorite food. Galen could eat it, but it was a long way from his favorite.

"Where will we go, Dad?" Nels asked as they headed south on

North Central Expressway. "I mean, do you think we can find a Mexican restaurant down here?"

"Oh, I don't know about that. I mean, what are the chances of finding a Mexican restaurant in Dallas? That might be hard," Galen teased.

Nels laughed. "Yeah, I guess we'll find one, all right." He leaned back in his seat. "Oh, wow," he said. "Look at all the lights down here."

Galen believed that the Dallas skyline was one of the most attractive night skylines in the nation. And one of the prettiest buildings was the forty-story office complex of Pangaea Oil. The Pangaea Building featured a lighted globe in red, white, and blue that took up fully a third of the building.

Interestingly, the globe did not portray the familiar continents of North and South America, but rather Pangaea, the supercontinent that geologists believe existed before the continental drift. Underneath the globe was the Pangaea motto: ENERGY BELONGS TO THE WORLD.

Galen turned off the Central Expressway onto Pangaea Drive. As he approached, the gate security man stepped up to the car.

"Galen Scobey," Galen said, showing his pass.

"Yes, sir," the guard said, looking at his clipboard. "You're meeting with Mr. Gleason?"

"Yes."

"And who is this big fella with you—your bodyguard?"

Nels laughed, then leaned forward to look at the security officer. "I'm his son," he said.

"Well, now, I don't know if I can let you in without some sort of title," the guard said, writing something on a little badge. "Would you be willing to be his bodyguard if that's the only way I can let you in?"

The boy nodded. "Yes, I'll be his bodyguard."

"Good, good, this should take care of it, then," the gate guard said. Smiling, he handed the temporary badge to Nels. "You need to wear that so everyone can see it, now."

"I will."

"Thanks," Galen said with a smile and a little wave as he drove on into the complex.

His meeting with CEO Bob Gleason was in the boardroom on the top floor. The view from up here was spectacular. As Galen settled into one of the comfortable leather chairs around the teak table, his son went over to look through the window.

"Are you going to be all right while I'm meeting with Mr. Gleason?" Galen asked.

Nels nodded. "I'll just look out at all the buildings."

At that moment another man came in. He was wearing a shirt and tie, but no jacket; his tie was loosened and his collar unbuttoned.

"Galen, forgive me for not meeting you when you arrived, but I was on the phone with the Secretary of the Interior."

"The secretary works this late?" Galen asked. "I'm impressed that the taxpayers are getting their money's worth."

"I called him at home," Gleason said. He passed off the remark as casually as if he had said that he just spoke with his brother. But such was the importance of Pangaea for the national energy grid that Bob Gleason could call not only the Interior secretary but those of Energy and State; once he even spoke with the vice president at his home.

"Any glitches?" Galen asked.

"No, and I intend to keep it that way," Gleason answered. He dropped a leather folder on the table, then sat down. Noticing Nels for the first time, he turned toward the boy and smiled. "Well, hello, Nels, it's good of you to come to the office."

"I had to come, Mr. Gleason. I'm Dad's bodyguard," Nels said, pointing to his badge.

"So you are," Gleason said. Then to Galen. "By the way, what are you going to do with Nels while you're gone?"

"Do with him? What do you mean, do with him? I plan to take him with me," Galen replied.

Gleason looked surprised. "You're taking him to the wilds of Alaska?"

"Hardly the wilds," Galen said. "I've done some research on Point Hope. It's a thriving little community, complete with a medical facility and a school. I plan to enroll him as soon as I arrive."

"Do you think that's wise?"

"Bob, Nels's mother died when he was only two years old. A lot of people have criticized me for not remarrying right away in order to give him a new mother, but I say that's a poor reason to get married. I've been mother and father to him for seven years now, and we've gotten along just fine."

Gleason held up his hand. "Whoa," he said. "I'm not being critical. In fact, I have nothing but admiration for you for being able to do it. More power to you, I say. Besides, you'll be up there through Christmas. I can see why you might want your son with you."

"Christmas has nothing to do with it."

"Of course it does. Everyone wants to be together through Christmas."

"I want to keep him with me all the time," Galen said. "Not just Christmas."

"Well, I can't argue with that."

"Sometimes it has been difficult," Galen admitted. "But in the end, it's well worth it."

"I'm sure it is. Well, let's get started, shall we?"

Gleason opened the folder and took out some papers. "Now here is all the authority you will need. This is a letter from the Department of Energy, granting us exclusive rights of exploration, this from the

Department of the Interior setting aside the environmental impact order, this from the Alaska Department of Environmental Protection, another from the North Slope Borough, and finally, this one from the mayor of Point Hope, all giving us access to the Point Hope Peninsula for oil exploration."

"Thanks." Galen picked up the documents. "You've made the first part of it easy. Now all I have to do is find some oil."

Suddenly and unexpectedly, there was a snapping sound, and the room went totally black as all the lights went out. A few seconds thereafter, the battery-powered emergency lights came on so that, once again, the room was lighted, though dimly.

"I'm glad we weren't in the elevator when that happened," Galen said. "I wonder if it's just this building?"

"No, Dad, it looks like the lights are out all over," Nels said. "Look at all the dark buildings."

"Must've blown a transformer somewhere."

Galen and Gleason walked over to join Nels at the window. The city wasn't totally dark, because here and there they could see the dim glow of emergency lamps, much like the battery-powered lamps they were using. But the bright lights that so identified Dallas's nighttime skyline were gone.

There was one exception to the darkness. Sitting atop Reunion Tower was a great, white ball of light, surrounded by a cluster of spearlike bars. This starburst was one of the most prominent landmarks of downtown Dallas, and while the rest of downtown was dark, the light over Reunion Tower still glowed brilliantly.

"Oh, wow, Dad, look!" Nels said, pointing. "It's like the Star of Bethlehem."

As Galen examined it, he thought it did look rather like a bright star that had descended from the heavens.

"I wonder why that's still on?" Galen asked.

"I don't know," Gleason said. "Maybe they have an emergency generator that comes on line when the power fails."

"Could be."

They heard several snaps and pops, then the building's ventilation system kicked on, rattled for a second, and held. At the same time, the lights came back up.

"Well, if it was a transformer, they sure got it fixed fast," Galen said.

"Or, more likely, they rerouted the grid," Gleason said. "So, you'll be leaving tomorrow?"

"Yes. Flying out of DFW for Seattle." Galen walked back to the table from the window. "Then from Seattle to Anchorage, Anchorage to Nome, to Kotzebue, and finally, a small plane into Point Hope."

"Sounds like a lot of flying."

"Yes, but we're used to it, aren't we, Nels?" Galen said.

Nels, sensing the meeting was about over, had come to stand beside his dad. Galen reached down to run his hand through his son's hair.

"We sure are," Nels said, proud that his father included him in such adult conversation.

Galen began singing the "Wandering Star" song from *Paint Your Wagon*. Happily, Nels joined in.

"All packed?" Galen asked, sticking his head into Nels's room.

"Yes. Hey, Dad, you know when we saw that Star of Bethlehem tonight?"

"What Star of Bethlehem?"

"You know, the one on top of Reunion Tower? How it didn't go out when all the other lights did?"

"Oh, yes. What about it?"

"It made me think of Mama."

"Oh? How?"

"Well, I can barely remember Mama, but I do remember her holding me and pointing to a really bright light."

Galen looked at Nels in surprise. "You can remember that?"

"Yes."

"You were only two years old."

"Then it *did* happen? She did hold me and point to a bright light?"

"Yes."

Nels smiled. "I'm glad I didn't just make that up. I don't remember anything else about it. I don't even know what the light was. I can just remember her holding me and pointing to it. And now, whenever I think of her, I remember that light."

"It was a star," Galen said.

"A star? Really? That's funny. In my memory it seems a lot brighter than a star."

"It wasn't a real star," Galen said. "It was a glass star, with a light inside. But you're right. It was very bright."

"Well, anyway, that's why the light on top of Reunion Tower reminds me of Mom."

"Yes, I suppose I can see that."

"You know what else reminds me of her?"

"What?"

"You know when we sing that song about being born under a wandering star? Well . . . I know it's probably dumb . . . but I've always sort of thought that Mom was that wandering star. You know . . . like . . . an angel guiding us or something."

Galen reached over and put his hand on Nels's shoulder, squeezing it affectionately.

"No, son, that's not dumb," he said. "That's not dumb at all. In fact, I think that is a very good way to remember your mother."

"I've looked at all the pictures and videos of Mom. She was very pretty, wasn't she, Dad?"

"Yes. She was beautiful."

"Do you miss her?"

"Yes, I miss her very much."

"I do too. I mean, even though I can barely remember her, I miss her. And you want to know when I miss her most?"

"When?"

"Around Christmas time. Like right now. You know, you see all these pictures of kids with their mom and dad at Christmas time. Except I don't have a mom. And that's when I miss her most."

"Yes," Galen agreed. "It is most difficult at Christmas."

"Dad, why don't we celebrate Christmas?"

"Well, we don't celebrate it because of what you just said."

"What do you mean?"

"Think about it, Nels," Galen said. "If there is something that makes you sad, then seeing everyone else very, very happy makes you even more sad."

"Oh, you mean, like, everyone is happy at Christmas with their mom and dad, but we're sad because Mom isn't here?"

"Yes. Now, you don't really want to have to go through all that, do you?"

"No, I guess not," Nels agreed.

"Besides, we'll be in Alaska this Christmas. And that's way up in the middle of nowhere. Chances are, when we get up there, you probably won't even know it's Christmas."

～ Three ～

Approaching Kotzebue, Alaska

"Cabin attendants, prepare the cabin for landing," the pilot's voice announced over the intercom.

There was a rumble and thump of landing gear being lowered as the attendants moved quickly up the aisle of the Boeing 737. Here and there they took a last-minute cup or napkin, while ensuring that all belts were fastened, trays stowed, and seatbacks in the upright position.

Nels was sitting next to the window, staring out at the ground below. "Dad, there's nothing down there but snow," he said. "No trees, no buildings, nothing."

"That's the tundra—or the ocean, I don't know which."

"Wow. You mean the ocean is frozen up here?"

"Yes."

"Cool."

Galen chuckled. "No, not just cool. It's *cold*," he said.

Nels laughed. "Come on, Dad, you know what I mean."

The plane was sinking lower and lower until finally the wheels touched down. A moment after touchdown Galen saw the thrust deflectors pop out on the engines, then there was the roar of applied power. The rapid deceleration forced him against his seatbelt. With taxi speed under control, the plane left the runway and taxied across the apron toward a small blue building.

"There's the terminal," Galen said.

"Boy, it sure isn't like DFW, is it?" Nels said. "It's real little."

"You have to remember, there aren't very many large cities up here."

"You know what I don't understand," Nels said. "How come little-bitty towns can get airline service? The real little towns back home don't get airline service."

"Well, that's because there are no highways or railroads up here. The only way to get from city to city is by air," Galen explained.

The plane came to a halt and an air-stair was pushed to the front door. About six people got up and started toward the front door.

"Dad, look at all the people out there."

Leaning down to look through the window, Galen saw that there was a rather substantial crowd waiting at the airport.

"Maybe someone famous is getting off the plane," Nels suggested.

Galen looked at the six people now standing by the door, waiting for it to be opened.

"I don't know," he said. "I don't see anyone I recognize."

The flight attendant, herself with the slightly Asiatic features of an Eskimo, opened the door, then stood beside it as each person left.

Galen was the last one to get off the plane.

"Were we carrying anyone important on this flight?" Galen asked.

The flight attendant smiled. "All of our passengers are important."

"No, I don't mean that. I mean, were we carrying anyone famous?"

"No, I don't think so. Why do you ask?"

"There seems to be a rather substantial crowd here at the airport."

The young woman laughed. "They meet every plane this way."

It had been sixty-five degrees Fahrenheit when they left Dallas.

When they landed, the pilot announced that the temperature on the ground at Kotzebue was minus twelve degrees. As Galen and Nels stepped out onto the air-stair, the cold hit them like a wall. Galen wasn't totally unprepared for the weather; he had made use of on-line shopping to outfit himself and Nels with down parkas, thermal trousers and underwear, as well as boots and gloves. But all that was packed away in his luggage, so for the moment they were both wearing jackets that were totally inadequate for the cold.

They hurried down the stairs, across the apron, and into the terminal building. Once inside, they found a hot-air vent and stood in front of it, letting the air blow over them until some of the chill was taken away.

A decorated Christmas tree stood in the middle of the terminal. In addition, there were Christmas decorations everywhere, including greenery and bright red bows. On the wall was a drawing of Santa Claus. But instead of riding in a red sleigh pulled by reindeer, he was standing on a sleigh being pulled by eight sled dogs.

Seeing the drawing, Nels laughed. "Dad, look. Up here, Santa Claus is in a dogsled."

Galen laughed as well. "Come to think of it, it makes more sense than being pulled by reindeer."

At that moment, a tall, slender, silver-haired man approached them.

"Would you be here from Pangaea Oil?" the man asked. "Is your name Galen Scobey?"

"Yes," Galen said.

The silver-haired man extended his hand. "Ah, good. Your company contacted me. I'm Bob Bivens. I'll be your pilot from here to Point Hope."

"You're the pilot?" Galen asked in surprise. "Do you meet all your passengers?"

"I sure do. Since I never have more than three or four at the most, it seems the mannerly thing to do." Bob pointed to the jacket Galen was wearing. "You got 'nything warmer'n that?"

"In our luggage we have parkas and all the rest."

"Uh-huh," Bivens said. "Well, Mr. Scobey, you might want to go ahead and claim your luggage now, so's you and the boy can put on somethin' warm. Else you're likely to freeze to death between here and the hotel."

"Between here and the hotel—what are you talking about? I thought we were flying on to Point Hope."

"We are, and we will," Bivens said. "Just as soon as the weather breaks up there. In the meantime, if you stay at Shellerbarger's Hotel, you get a special rate, seein' as you're my passenger.

"Me 'n Gladys Shellerbarger are what you might call tight," Bivens added. "So she does that for my customers."

"I see. Who else does she do it for?"

Bivens laughed and pointed his finger at Galen. "Well, pard, you got me there. Truth to tell, ole Gladys will do that for anyone who asks her."

Bivens walked over to the baggage claim area with them and Galen started pulling out his luggage. He had five pieces.

"Whoa. There's just you and the boy, isn't there?"

"That's all. Why?"

"Look, you won't be the only thing I'll be taking up to Point Hope," Bivens explained. "I've got some goods for the Native Store. We're goin' to be pretty crowded as it is, then you start pilin' in all this extra luggage, it's going to be all I can do to get ole *Saigon Sue* off the ground."

"Who is *Saigon Sue*?" Nels asked.

"Well, young fella, *Saigon Sue* is my airplane," Bivens said. "She's a twin-engine Beechcraft, D-18. I named her *Saigon Sue* after a pretty Vietnamese girl I met back in Saigon."

Galen and Nels began putting on their parkas and cold-weather gear. As they did so, they drew stares. It was obvious to almost everyone in the airport terminal that these were novices from the lower forty-eight.

"If you're all bundled up now, I'll take you to the hotel," Bivens offered.

"What about our luggage?"

"Have you got some things in one bag? I mean, things you'll need just to spend a night or two?"

"Yes, that one." Galen pointed to the smallest suitcase.

"Okay, grab that one and put all the rest into a locker. I'll take you down to Shellerbarger's."

"You have a car outside?"

"A car?" Bivens laughed.

"Oh, yeah, up here I figure all you guys have SUVs or pickup trucks."

"Try snowmobile."

Bivens led them outside. Again the cold air hit with all the impact of a brick wall, but at least this time they were prepared for it.

They were prepared for the cold, but not for what they saw in the parking lot. There were scores of snowmobiles, with very few cars, SUVs, or pickup trucks in sight.

"That's mine," Bivens said, pointing to a yellow snowmobile.

"Surely you don't expect us all to fit on that thing?" Galen protested.

"Oh we'll make it," Bivens replied easily. "We'll just put the boy in the middle, to keep him from sliding off."

They followed Bivens over to the bright yellow snowmobile. He unplugged the little engine heater, then settled Galen and Nels before starting the engine.

After an exhilarating ride of no more than a mile, they stopped in front of a two-story metal frame building. A sign over the porch read: SHELLERBARGER'S HOTEL AND NATIVE ARTS GIFT STORE.

"Come on inside, I'll help you get registered."

The building was divided into two parts. One side was obviously a store. It actually reminded Galen of a small country store he had once seen, long ago, near his grandmother's house. The other side was a somewhat more open area, with a couple of round tables near a stove. At the back of the room was a counter, and behind the counter, a woman was writing on a yellow tablet.

"Hey, Gladys, quit counting your money and come take care of your customers," Bivens called.

"Hah, don't I wish I was counting my money." Gladys laughed, putting the tablet to one side and standing up. She looked to be in her mid-fifties, only slightly overweight. Her hair was drawn back in a bun, and she had a pencil sticking in it, just over her ear. She was round-faced, but clearly not an Eskimo.

"You must be the Scobeys," she greeted, smiling at Galen as he approached the counter.

"Has my picture been plastered all over Alaska? How is it that everyone knows me by name?"

"Well, let's see. A new fella is coming to look for oil, and he's bringing his nine-year-old son with him. From the looks of the outfit you're wearing, I would say it—and you—are new." She pointed to Nels. "And unless I miss my guess, you would be about nine years old."

"Nine and a half," Nels said.

"Nine years and four months," Galen corrected.

"Well, that's almost nine and a half."

"I've got a room for you upstairs," Gladys said. "You are welcome to it as long as the weather stays bad."

"Thanks. Oh, what about meals? Is there a restaurant in town?"

"You're standing in as fine a restaurant as there is in Kotzebue," Bivens insisted. "What are we having tonight, Gladys?"

"Reindeer stew."

"Reindeer stew? This close to Christmas? Don't you feel a little guilty about that?" Bivens teased.

"Nah, everybody knows Santa Claus uses dogsleds up here," Gladys said.

"Anyway, you've served reindeer stew for the last three days."

"You don't have to eat it, you know."

"Oh, I'm going to eat it, all right. I was just pointing that out to you, is all."

"This is the third day I've served it because I still have part of that hind quarter that I got from Raleigh Touksauk. I figure on using all of it up before I start on anything else."

Without being invited, Bob Bivens joined Galen and Nels at the supper table that night.

"I just checked on the weather," he said. "Doesn't look good over the next twenty-four hours." He fished an oversized cracker from the basket that sat on the table. A moment later, without having ordered, his meal was delivered. He made liberal use of hot sauce.

"Boy, you sure like hot sauce," Nels said.

Bivens chuckled. "Don't get me wrong, I think Gladys's reindeer stew is as good as you can find anywhere. But after three days of it, a little hot sauce makes it go down easier."

Galen added a little hot sauce to his own plate. "What's your story, Mr. Bivens?" he asked.

"My story?"

"You aren't native to Alaska, are you? I mean, you certainly aren't an Eskimo."

Bivens laughed again. "No, I reckon not. Not much of a story, really. Like a lot of guys who came back from Vietnam, I didn't find it all that easy to settle back into civilian life. I began drifting around for a while, then heard about bush flying in Alaska from an old buddy of mine. So, I bought this airplane, and here I am. I've been here now for twenty-five years."

Galen looked up from his meal. "Wait a minute. You mean the airplane you'll be flying us in is twenty-five years old?" he asked with some trepidation.

Bivens chuckled. "Heavens no."

Galen breathed a sigh of relief. "That's good."

"It's almost fifty years old," Bivens said. This time he laughed out loud.

"We're supposed to fly in an airplane that's fifty years old?"

"There are still airlines flying DC-3s," Bivens explained. "Some of those airplanes are seventy years old. And they say that the B-52 may be around for one hundred years."

"I had no idea airplanes could last that long."

"The only reason cars don't last that long is because it would wreck our economy not to have new models coming out every year," Bivens said.

"So, where do you live now?"

"Kotzebue and Point Hope."

"Wait a minute, you live in Kotzebue *and* Point Hope?" Galen asked.

"Yeah. Weather keeps me on the ground there about as often as it does here."

"Here you go, Bob." Gladys came to the table with a tray on which there were three plates. "Apple pie for you and your passengers. Tonight it's on the house."

"Well, thank you," Galen said.

"Ah, think nothing of it," Gladys said with a dismissive wave of her hand. "Tomorrow you'll be wanting some more and you'll have to buy it. And I'll charge you twice as much." She laughed out loud as she started back toward the check-in counter.

"She'll do it, too," Bivens said.

"Uhmm," Galen said, taking a bite of his apple pie. "This is very good."

"Yeah," Bivens said, taking a bite of his own pie. "It just doesn't get any better than this."

Galen and Nels spent two more days in Kotzebue. On the third day, they were awakened by a banging on their door.

"Yes, wait," Galen said, getting out of bed and picking his way through the dark to the door. When he opened it, Bob Bivens was standing there, smiling broadly.

"Today's the day."

"What time is it?"

"It's about eight."

Galen shook his head. "Eight o'clock, and it's pitch dark outside. I'm having a hard time getting used to this cycle of light and dark."

"Everyone does at first, but you learn to adjust. I'll have Gladys fix your breakfast."

"Thanks," Galen said. "We'll be down soon."

~ *Four* ~

Point Hope

Galen and Nels shared the airplane with crates of tomatoes and let-
tuce, and their luggage. As they let down from the low-lying clouds,
they descended onto a scene that looked as if it had been bypassed
by time. Ice was jammed against a rocky beach where small boats
of wood and sealskin were stacked on shore. Galen pointed to the
boats.

"Yes," Bivens shouted over the noise of the engines. "During whaling season, the whalers go out in those boats to catch the bowheads."

"Bowheads?"

"Whales," Bivens explained.

"What do you mean, catching whales? Do they count them, or
what?"

"No, they go out after them and they kill them. Point Hope is one
of the few places where you can still do that," Bivens said.

As they continued their approach toward the Point Hope airport,
Galen saw a fenced-off area, marked with what looked like large,
white curved boards. He asked Bivens about it.

"That's the cemetery," Bivens replied. "The graves are marked by whalebones; the bigger the bones, the more important the whaling captain who is buried there."

"Interesting," Galen said.

The wheels of the Twin Beech touched down smoothly and Bivens taxied them toward the little terminal building. That was when they saw a four-engined airplane, nose-down on a collapsed landing gear.

"What is that?"

"That's a Lockheed Electra that didn't quite make it."

"When did it happen?"

"About thirty years ago."

"Thirty years ago? And it's still here?"

Bivens chuckled. "What are they going to do with it?"

"Look at this terminal, Nels," Galen said. "And you thought the terminal in Kotzebue was small."

When Bivens killed the engines, Galen and Nels got up from their seats, picked their way through the crowded aisle to the cabin door, then climbed down from the plane. They were somewhat better prepared for the cold this time than when they arrived at Kotzebue.

"Don't worry about your luggage," Bivens said. "I'll get it delivered for you."

"Thanks. And, if I don't see you again, it has been interesting," Galen said, shaking hands.

"Oh, you'll see me again. When the weather allows it, I come here about three times a week."

Galen and Nels hurried on across the hard-packed, snow-covered apron and into the little Quonset hut that served as the airport terminal. Like the terminal in Kotzebue, this one was decorated for Christmas, complete with tree, artificial greenery, and a large crèche.

"They do celebrate Christmas here," Galen said as he looked with disapproval at the extravagant decorations.

A short man with Eskimo features walked toward them.

"Mr. Scobey?"

"Yes."

"I'm Mark Hale."

"Hale?"

Hale nodded. "Not all Eskimos have Eskimo names," he said. "Though, of course, if you go far enough into our background, we do. Luke Koonook sent me to meet you."

"Koonook," Galen said, stumbling over the name. "Yes, I recognize the name. He is your mayor, I believe?"

"He is. Mr. Bivens said he would take care of your luggage?"

"He did."

"Good. Then if you'll come with me, I'll take you to where you are going to stay."

There was no parking lot as such, but there was a Jeep pulled up against the side of the administration building. Hale unplugged the engine heater and motioned for Galen and Nels to get in. "Then you can meet with the mayor."

"I'm surprised to see a car," Galen said.

Hale chuckled. "We have a few cars and pickups. But mostly we use ATVs and snowmobiles. This one belongs to the mayor. He wanted to get a Lincoln Navigator, but his wife talked him into settling for a used Jeep."

Galen got in the right seat and Nels crawled into the back. Hale drove away slowly to avoid pedestrians and snowmobiles.

"So," he said. "I understand you're going to discover oil and make everyone in Point Hope rich."

"Oh, I don't know about that," Galen replied, not sure by the tone of Hale's voice whether he was hopeful, joking, or sarcastic.

"That's what our esteemed mayor said when he sold this program to the council," Hale said.

"He had to sell it to the council? Was it a difficult sale?"

Hale nodded. "Very difficult," he said. "It passed by only one vote."

"I didn't know that."

"My vote," Hale added. "And I originally voted against it."

"What won you over? The promise of riches?" Galen asked jokingly.

"No. To tell you the truth, Mr. Scobey, I don't believe for one minute there is anything out there, but I know folks are going to come looking, so I figure it's better to let one man come up here and look for it, rather than bring up an entire army of people, tramping around on the tundra, disrupting the ecosystem."

"What ecosystem is there to disrupt?" Galen asked. "From all the pictures I've seen, there's nothing out there but clumps of moss."

"There is an ecosystem there, and it's quite fragile," Hale said quietly. "I would hope that whatever investigative method you use takes that into account."

"I'll be drilling some holes to run tests," Galen said. "But after I've left, you'll hardly know I was here."

"And if you discover something, what then?"

"That will be the next stage of operation. I'm in the finding business, not the drilling business. But we do have new drilling techniques that leave a very small footprint."

"What do you mean?"

"All right, it's not like the pictures you see of the old oil fields in the early days down in Texas and Oklahoma, where there was a forest of derricks. Today we can crowd hundreds of wells into a very small area. One bit can thread its way to several deposits using the same bore, which means that they spread out underground in all directions."

"I hope you're right," Hale said. "I can't imagine a bigger shame than looking out to see something like that."

"Is that the school?" Nels asked, as they drove past a building that was considerably more substantial than any other they could see.

"That's it," Hale said.

"As soon as we get settled in, I'll take you down to get enrolled," Galen promised.

"It's not very big," Nels said.

"Well, then, it shouldn't take you long to learn everybody's name, should it?" Galen replied, putting the best light on it.

Hale stopped in front of a building with a sign reading GUS KOWANNA'S BED AND BREAKFAST.

"We have a motel called the Whalers' Inn," he said. "But if you're going to be in Point Hope for any length of time, I think you'll be more comfortable here. A lot of hunters stay here when they come. This is practically Bob Bivens's second home and pilots who get weathered in stay here as well. Come on in, I'll introduce you to the Kowannas. They're the people who run the place."

"Thanks."

Like the airport, the bed and breakfast was elaborately decorated for Christmas.

A man and a woman were sitting in the middle of the room by an oil-burning stove. Both had dark hair, eyes, and Eskimo features. The man was carving something white and the woman was reading a book. The woman, who was short and round, stood up when they came in.

"Mr. Scobey, welcome to Point Hope," she said. She stuck out her hand. "And welcome to you too, Nelson."

"People call me Nels."

"Well then, I will call you Nels too, if that is all right," she said. "I'm Molly, and this person who doesn't have the manners to stand up and greet you is Gus."

"If I stop right now, I'll lose track of where I am," Gus protested.

Nels walked over to look. "What are you making?" he asked.

"An ivory polar bear," Gus said, showing it.

"Oh, cool!" Nels said. "Dad, come look."

Galen came over. There was nothing amateurish about Gus's work. It was beautifully carved and intricate in every detail.

"That's very good," Galen said. He examined it more closely. "That's more than very good, that is outstanding. Have you had training?"

"My father put a file in my hand before I could walk," he said. "He was a carver, as was his father before him, and *his* father before him. It is said that when the first white men came to Point Hope, they traded whiskey and tobacco for my great-great-grandfather's carvings."

"We would be better off if he had traded for something other than whiskey and tobacco," Molly said. "Come, I'll show you your room."

"Thank you."

Galen and Nels followed Molly down a hallway to a room at the back of the building.

"This will be your room," she said proudly. "As you can see, it has two beds, and a TV. If you need a table or a desk, I'll have Gus bring one in for you. Also, I'll have him bring in a small Christmas tree. Just because you're away from home is no reason why you can't celebrate Christmas."

"We don't celebrate Christmas," Galen said.

"Oh. Are you Jewish?"

"No."

"What are you?"

"Ethnically, I suppose you could say I am Christian. I mean, I was born Christian, but . . . "

"Ethnically?" Molly asked. She made a small harrumphing sound in the back of her throat. "There is no such thing as an ethnic Christian," she said. "You either are Christian, or you aren't."

"Yes," Galen answered, anxious to change the subject. "Well, a table that could double as a desk would be fine."

"I'll see that you have one. Along with a Christmas tree," she added, pointedly. Then she continued her guided tour of the room. "The heat comes through the vents. Only one control and we have that. But you'll not get too cold. Just down the hall you'll find running water."

"It's good to see that you have running water," Galen replied. "I was wondering about that."

"Well, we don't actually have running water, but we do have a holding tank," Molly explained. "We hope to get running water some day, and a sewer system. Now we use honey buckets."

Nels laughed. "We know what honey buckets are, don't we, Dad?"

"Yes we do," Galen replied.

"How do you know about honey buckets?" Molly asked.

"We used them in Venezuela."

"You've been to Venezuela?"

"I've been everywhere. Haven't I, Dad?"

"Pretty much," Galen agreed. Then, to Molly, "Oh, if you recall, in the letter I sent, I asked if you would find someone to look out for Nels on those times I might not be around."

"I can look out for myself, Dad," Nels complained.

"Yes, in Dallas maybe. But up here, I would feel it would be better if there was someone who knew the ropes a little more."

"I'll look out for him," Molly said. She smiled at Nels. "I won't make a pest of myself, I promise. But I'm going to be here anyway. And I'll already be cooking the meals. So, you see, it will almost be as if you're looking out for yourself."

"Oh," Nels said. "Okay."

Mark Hale knocked on the door. "Mr. Scobey, would you like to come meet the mayor now?"

"I expect I should do that," Galen replied. "Nels, how about you stay here and look after our luggage when it arrives?"

"Which bed do you want, Dad?"

"I'll let you choose. You're in charge of quarters."

"Okay. I'll have everything all ready when you get back."

Luke Koonook was not only the best hunter in town, he was also a whaling captain, and the mayor. He was watching television when Hale brought Galen in. The mayor picked up a remote and muted the sound, though the picture of the newscaster, along with the scroll along the bottom, continued.

"Satellite TV," the mayor explained. "We didn't have any of that when I was a kid, growing up here. In fact, we barely had radio. Now, I don't know what I would do without Fox News, CNN, MSNBC. They keep us up to the minute with the rest of the world." He looked up at Hale. "Did you get them checked in?"

"Yes," Galen said, answering for Hale. "I left Nels with Mrs. Kowanna."

"Well, he couldn't be in any better hands than with Molly," Koonook said. "So, how soon do you expect to get started on your exploration?"

"Right away," Galen said. "I'll need to hire a guide."

"My dad will be your guide," Hale said. "His name is Amos."

"Uh, no offense," Galen replied. "But how old is your father? The work could become pretty physical."

To Galen's surprise, both Hale and Koonook laughed.

"What is it? What's funny?"

"Amos Hale has participated in the Iditarod for ten of the last twelve years," Koonook said. "And last year, he came in eighth out of forty-seven finishers. That's over a thousand miles."

Galen chuckled. "I guess I put my foot in my mouth," he said. "I'd be proud to have your father working with me. Now, what about transportation?"

"Only three kinds of transportation for the tundra," Koonook replied. "ATV, snowmobile, and dogsled."

"Dogsled?" Galen laughed. "That's fine for Mr. Hale, but I don't think I'm ready for that yet. I was thinking I might have a four-wheel-drive vehicle brought up. Rather like your Jeep."

"We have less than two miles of road in all of Point Hope," Koonook said. "Are you planning on looking for oil on one of those streets?"

"Well, no, but . . . "

"No buts about it," Koonook said. "You can't use an SUV out on the tundra. You could use an ATV but, being that it's winter, you'd be a lot better off with a snowmobile."

"All right. Do you think you could locate one for me?"

"I already have."

Galen chuckled. "I hope you also have someone who can teach me how to drive it."

"Won't take you a minute to learn," Koonook said.

"Good. I appreciate all you've done so far."

"Now, I want you to do something for me," Koonook said.

"What is that?"

"Tonight, around seven, we're going to have a meeting at the school gymnasium. I would like for you to come talk about what you are going to be doing up here."

Galen looked surprised. "Why do I need to do that? I thought all this was already taken care of." He opened his briefcase and took out a file folder. "I've got letters of authorization here from everyone who has any interest in the project, from the federal government all the way down to, well, you."

"Yes, and I'm all for what you are doing," Koonook said. "But it would help if you would come talk to these people."

"At the school gymnasium?"

"Yes."

Galen nodded. "All right, if you think it is necessary. Actually, I need to go down to the school now, anyway. I want to get Nels enrolled in class."

"He'll be in Ellie Springer's class," Koonook said. "She's a fine lady."

When Galen and Nels walked into the school office, Sam Keating was in conversation with a young Eskimo woman. Looking up as Galen entered, he smiled and stepped toward him with his hand extended.

"Mr. Scobey, I'm Sam Keating, principal of Tikigaq School," he said. "Welcome to Point Hope."

"I have to tell you, I've never been anywhere in my life before where I was so universally recognized. It's almost as if I were some celebrity," Galen said.

Sam laughed. "It isn't that you're universally recognized," he said. "It's that you *aren't* recognized."

"I beg your pardon?"

"Well, everybody up here knows everybody else. So, if we are expecting someone new, and we see someone we don't know, we know immediately who they are. Uh—if that makes sense to you."

"Actually, it does make sense to me," Galen said. He laughed. "Maybe I'm already getting acclimated."

Sam looked at Nels. "Nelson, welcome to our school."

"Thank you," Nels said.

"This is Sunshine Komack," Sam said, introducing Galen and Nels to the young Eskimo woman he was talking to. "She's one of our teachers' assistants."

"Are you going to be my teacher?" Nels asked.

"No," Sunshine said. "Your teacher will be Miss Springer."

"Ellie Springer," Sam said. "Like you, she's from Dallas."

"Dallas is where our home is, but we live everywhere, don't we, Dad?" Nels said proudly.

"Just about," Galen agreed. "In my profession I travel a lot and, as often as I can, I take Nels with me. This time last year, we were in Saudi Arabia. We were there for eighteen months, and before that we were in Venezuela."

"Oh my, then I'm sure you will be a big help to Miss Springer during geography lessons," Sam said to Nels. Then to Galen, "Mr. Scobey, I'm sure you will want to meet the teacher as well, so, why don't you just go with Sunshine. After Nelson—"

"—Nels," Nels said.

"Okay, I'll remember that. After Nels is settled in, you can come back here and we'll take care of his enrollment. I'm looking forward to the meeting tonight."

"You know about that as well?"

"In a village as small as Point Hope, if someone itches, we all scratch," Sam said.

~ Five ~

Like everyone in Point Hope, Ellie Springer was aware that the giant oil company, Pangaea, would be conducting tests in the area. She remembered the Pangaea Building, having driven by it many times on the Central Expressway. It was a pretty building and its presence was welcomed in Dallas because of the number of jobs it provided.

But, like other huge petroleum companies, Pangaea had a rather checkered past with regard to its environmental impact. She remembered, vaguely, a lawsuit involving Pangaea's use of a depleted oil field as a site of toxic waste injection. The lawsuit alleged that the toxic wastes leeched into the aquifer, and a rather substantial out-of-court settlement seemed to validate the claim.

Though some extolled the benefits that a big oil discovery would bring, Ellie believed that the negatives outweighed the positives. She feared that it would be the end of Point Hope's unique status. The population would explode, the culture would be changed forever, and the damage to the environment might be irreparable.

But because she realized that she was an outsider, she was making it a point to stay out of it. She considered it a local matter and, while she felt comfortably at home in Point Hope, she had no intention of spending the rest of her life here, so she didn't believe she had any right to add her own opinion to what was becoming a very hot issue.

Ellie had just given her class some seatwork and they were busy with the assignment when Sunshine Komack stuck her head in through the door.

"Miss Springer?"

"Yes, Miss Komack."

"I have a new student for you." Sunshine opened the door wider and motioned for Nels to come in. The boy stepped into the room and looked around in nervous curiosity.

"Ahh, *nalokme*," one of the children said.

"*Nalokme*," another agreed, and the word was repeated several times.

"*Nalokme*, yes, he is not a native," Ellie said. "Children, this is Nelson Scobey. I want you all to welcome him."

"Welcome, Nelson," the class said in unison.

"He wants to be called Nels," Sunshine said.

"Then Nels it shall be," Ellie said. "And you would be Nels's father," she added, noticing Galen, who had come into the room at the same time but hesitated just at the door.

"Yes," Galen said.

"Miss Komack, would you find a seat for Nels? Then have the class stand, one at a time, and introduce themselves to him."

"Yes, Miss Springer," Sunshine said.

While that was going on, Ellie invited Galen to step out into the hall with her. She closed the door behind her, then stuck her hand out.

"Welcome to Point Hope," she said, smiling broadly at him.

"Thank you. What was that word I heard the children saying when Nels was introduced?"

"Nalokme," Ellie said. "It's what the Eskimos call those who aren't native." She smiled. "It isn't pejorative."

"Ah, good. I wouldn't want Nels to have to undergo any more stress than is normal from a move as radical as the one he just made."

"You came here from Dallas?" Ellie asked.

"Yes. I understand you're from Dallas as well?"

"North Dallas, near the intersection of Preston and Campbell, if you're familiar with the area."

"Yes, I know the area quite well. Uh, Miss Springer, could I ask you a question?"

"Of course you can."

"Before coming up here, did you teach in Dallas?"

"Yes, I taught for two years at Brentwood Elementary."

"How would you compare this school with, say, Brentwood Elementary?"

"Well, that's a difficult question. It's a little like comparing apples and oranges . . . ," Ellie started, but before she could continue, Galen held up his hand.

"No, Miss Springer, comparing the quality of education there with here is not comparing apples and oranges," he interrupted. "And the *quality* of education is what I'm interested in."

"You are concerned about Nels's education?"

"Yes, of course I am."

"Then, if you don't mind my asking, if you are concerned that he may not get as good an education here as he was getting in Dallas, why didn't you leave him in Dallas? Surely your mission here won't be very long."

"I brought him with me because there is no one to leave him with in Dallas. His mother died when he was very young."

"Oh, I'm sorry to hear that," Ellie said.

"And I want him with me," Galen added. He smiled. "He's not only my son, he's my partner. We're a team, Nels and I."

Ellie returned the smile. "Well, I must say that I like that attitude in a parent," she said. "All right, Mr. Scobey, I'll be as frank as I can be. In some ways, we may be even better than the Dallas school system. Because of the state's oil revenue, all of the schools in the state are exceptionally well funded. That means we can have anything we need, from an individual computer for each student to sports equipment to teachers."

Galen chuckled. "Teachers? You mean that issue was in doubt?"

"It was before the influx of oil money," Ellie said. "There weren't enough teachers to have one per grade, so nearly every teacher taught multiple grades in the same classroom. Today, every class has its own teacher, and some classes have more than one teacher."

"I see."

"That also has the advantage of keeping the class-to-teacher ratio low, so there's a lot of one-on-one instruction when it is needed."

"Yes, I can see the advantage to that," Galen said. "So, it is your opinion that the schools up here are superior to the schools in Dallas?"

Ellie shook her head. "No, I didn't say that. If you recall, I said you were comparing apples and oranges. Each school has its own unique set of circumstances and advantages. What Dallas has, and what we lack, is a diverse environment."

"A diverse environment? I'm not sure what you mean by that."

"In a single classroom in Dallas you will find white children, black children, Hispanics, and Asians. You will have children from some of the wealthiest families as well as children who barely know where their next meal is coming from. And, of course, you will also have children who have diverse religious backgrounds. Here, everyone is Christian."

"Yes, so I've noticed," Galen replied. "I've never seen an entire town with such a public proclamation of their religious affiliation. There are signs of Christmas everywhere."

"That's true," Ellie replied. "One of the things you'll learn here is just how important Christmas is to the people of Point Hope. But, to continue with the comparison, Dallas is also rich in cultural opportunities; museums, concerts, art shows." She laughed. "Yes, and even the Cowboys, Rangers, and Mavericks. We have none of that up here, Mr. Scobey, and we never will have. Most of my kids have never seen a bridge, a train, or an interstate highway. They've never been to a movie theater, or visited a large department store. They have no concept of flushing a toilet or what it is like to have an endless supply of running water." She held up her finger. "But those things, Mr. Scobey, are part of a diverse environment, they are not part of a school curriculum."

Galen smiled broadly. "As you said, apples and oranges." He nodded. *"Touché."*

"I don't think you will be disappointed, Mr. Scobey," Ellie said. "I'm sure you don't plan to become a permanent resident. So, consider your time up here as a way of adding to the already rich tapestry of experiences for Nels."

Galen chuckled and nodded. "You should work for the school board's chamber of commerce . . . if there is such a thing," he said. "You've convinced me that Nels will learn a lot while he's here."

"And we will learn from him. I look forward to having him in class."

"Oh, and I'm glad you have such a positive attitude about the advantages of oil exploration."

"But I don't," Ellie said.

Galen looked confused. "You don't? I thought you just said your school had benefited economically from the oil production."

"That's true, we have. And I confess to being somewhat of a

hypocrite along those lines. I use, enjoy, and appreciate the money that oil production has made available to the school systems. As long as that oil production is somewhere else. I wouldn't want to see it on Tikigaq. If I had my way, you wouldn't be here at all."

"Wouldn't you like to see the citizens of Point Hope have some of the benefits a thriving oil economy could provide for them?"

"I'm not sure that the benefits outweigh the harm."

"The harm?"

"You haven't forgotten the *Exxon Valdez,* have you?" Ellie said quietly.

"No, Miss Springer, I haven't forgotten the *Exxon Valdez.* But that was a one-time incident."

"One time is all it takes."

"Yes. Well, I'm sorry you feel that way," Galen said. "Uh, perhaps I'd better let you get back to your class now. Thank you for meeting with me this morning."

"All part of the job, Mr. Scobey. And I'll see you tonight."

"You'll see me tonight?"

"Yes. Aren't you supposed to be at the school gymnasium at seven tonight?"

"Oh, yes, I believe the mayor did say something about that. You mean you'll be coming to that?"

"I wouldn't miss it for the world," Ellie said, smiling at him.

"No, given your feelings about this, I guess you wouldn't."

"Trust me, I am not your adversary, Mr. Scobey. You will have a few tonight, but I will not be one of them. Enjoy your stay in Point Hope," she said, as she opened the door to her classroom.

She was a pretty thing, Galen thought. It was too bad she already had an unfavorable opinion of him.

"Thanks, I will." Glancing through the open door, Galen saw that two or three kids had already gathered around Nels. He hoped the animosity some felt toward his mission here wouldn't manifest itself in hostility toward Nels. But Nels was an old hand at this, able to make friends quickly. Truth be known, Galen thought, Nels will probably fare a lot better here than I will.

Galen arrived at the school gym at about a quarter to seven. He had thought he would be talking to the city council members and, at most, a few more interested parties. He was shocked to see that the gym was filled with people, for the entire village of Point Hope had turned out to hear what he had to say.

Luke Koonook met him, then took him inside and up onto the stage where there were several folding chairs.

"Have a seat," Koonook said. "I'll introduce you."

"Mayor, what is the entire town doing here?" Galen asked. "I thought I was just going to be talking to a few interested people."

"Well, you have to understand that in a place as small as Point Hope, any diversion from normal is excitement. If you were here to-night to talk about the migratory habits of the Appalachian Bluebird, you would have a full auditorium. But in this case, the people are more interested than normal, since this affects each and every one of them."

As Galen took his seat on the stage, he looked around the gym. On one wall he saw the words TIKIGAQ HARPOONERS, written in black and outlined in gold. There was also a drawing of the team mascot, an Eskimo whaler, wearing a parka with a bushy fur hood. The whaler was standing in the front of a boat with a harpoon raised over his shoulder, in the throwing position. The gym floor lines were black, and the paint in the three-second zone was gold.

He also saw Christmas greenery hanging from the gym walls and realized that, clearly, there was little or no regard for the concept of separation of church and state up here.

Koonook stepped to the podium, held his hands up, and called for quiet. The buzz of conversation stilled and all faces stared toward the front.

"Thank you for coming to this meeting," Koonook began. "As all of you know, Pangaea Oil Company thinks there might be oil here, and Mr. Galen Scobey has come up to find it."

"We don't want any drilling up here!" someone shouted from the audience.

"Are you crazy?" another shouted back. "If they find oil up here, we're all going to be rich."

"Some things are more important than money!" the first man shouted.

"Please, please," Koonook said, holding out his hands in a plea for order. "You are all going to get your opportunity to ask Mr. Scobey questions."

"Questions?" Galen asked, turning toward Mark Hale, who was sitting next to him.

Mark chuckled. "What you are seeing here, Mr. Scobey, is true democracy in action. We are small enough in number that when there is something significant that affects us, everyone has a voice."

"Nobody told me there would be questions."

"Mr. Scobey?" Koonook said from the podium.

Looking toward the podium, Galen saw the mayor smiling, and extending his hand toward him.

"Would you come over and say a few words, please?"

Clearing his throat, Galen moved toward the podium. Gripping each side of it almost as if it were a life preserver, he cleared his throat again and looked out over the audience. All eyes were on him, and scattered throughout the audience were flashes of light reflecting from the glasses of those who wore them. He cleared his throat again. He should've told Koonook that he didn't do speeches.

"I . . . uh," he started, only to be interrupted by an ear-piercing screech from the PA system.

"Henry!" Koonook shouted.

Henry Killigivuk, the school janitor, jumped up from his chair and rushed to some spot just offstage. The screeching stopped.

Galen waited a moment, then he started again. "I am glad to be here, representing Pangaea in their search for oil. And I want to thank the mayor and others for their warm welcome. Thank you."

Galen started to sit down.

"Wait, aren't you going to answer any questions?" someone shouted from the audience.

Reluctantly, Galen returned to the podium. "I will answer them if I can," he said.

"Are you really going to make everyone in Point Hope rich? Or was that just a way of getting us to cooperate?"

"And you are?" Galen asked.

"George Komack."

"Well, Mr. Komack, I'm quite sure that Pangaea didn't promise to make anyone rich, and I'm certainly making no such promises."

"Then what are you here for?"

"I am here to conduct some tests, to see if there is any justification for exploratory drilling."

"Exploratory drilling," Komack replied. "And what, exactly, is exploratory drilling?"

"All drilling is exploratory until oil is hit," Galen replied.

"So, what you are saying is, even if you give Pangaea the go-ahead, and they begin drilling, there's still no guarantee that there will be oil?"

Galen laughed nervously. "Mr. Komack, if I could guarantee oil, I would be richer than Bill Gates. I can only suggest whether or not the signs justify further exploration."

"So, based entirely upon your word, we might have a lot of drilling going on out there," Komack said. "We could see the total destruction of our ecosystem, to say nothing of our culture, and get nothing for it. And all of this, Mr. Scobey, based upon what you recommend."

Galen brushed a fall of hair back from his forehead. "You are putting a lot of pressure on me, Mr. Komack," he said with a little laugh. "Is that your intention?"

"It is," Komack answered without reservation. "I want you to be fully aware of the consequences of your action."

"Are you a patriotic man, Mr. Komack? Because if you are, then you are aware of our country's need to be less dependent upon foreign sources for our oil. You could look at this as your patriotic duty."

"I served in Vietnam as my patriotic duty," Komack said. "I am loyal to our nation, Mr. Scobey. But I'm also loyal to a greater cause. I am a patriot of the future."

The crowd cheered.

Komack pointed toward the east. "Go five miles in that direction and the land looks exactly as it did ten thousand years ago. Can you tell me that, as a result of what you are doing now, it will look the same ten thousand years from now?"

"Mr. Komack, I think any damage to the environment will be minimal. Certainly during the exploratory stage, and even if oil is discovered. As for changing your culture if oil is discovered and developed, well, I can't speak to that. That will be in your hands. But I do know that my time here will have absolutely no impact on your environment, or your culture."

"That's where you are wrong, Mr. Scobey," Komack said. "It all starts with you, and if I had my way, you'd be on the next plane out of Point Hope."

There were more cheers.

Mark Hale stood up then. His words were not addressed to Galen but to the audience.

"I think that some of you, perhaps most of you, know that, in many ways, I agree with George Komack," he began. "I do not want to look out my window and see oil wells."

Komack's supporters cheered, and Mark held his hands up in a call for quiet.

"But," he said, "you may also know that I voted in favor of granting Mr. Scobey permission to search."

"Why'd you do that, Mark, if you are against it?" someone called.

"Because if he doesn't do it, someone else will. In fact, they might even start this exploratory drilling that Mr. Scobey was talking about, without so much as a preliminary survey. And if they do that and find nothing, we will have all the evil of an oil field without any of the benefits. On the other hand, if Mr. Scobey's survey turns up negative, then we will be left in peace. I say, let him do his job. I'm confident there's nothing out there, and I believe him when he says that we will hardly know he's here."

Mark's words were even more favorably received than George Komack's had been, because his were the words of reason. Both sides of the issue could support him. There were a few more questions and comments, but when the meeting ended, the general consensus was to let Galen do his job.

Koonook returned to the podium to address the audience. "Before we leave, Father Tobin has asked me to remind those of you who are part of the Christmas planning committee to meet with him at St. Thomas's as soon as we are finished here."

"Well, are we finished, Luke?" someone asked, and the audience laughed.

"We are," Koonook said.

~ *Six* ~

The next morning Galen woke up and, looking at the clock, saw that it was after nine.

"Nels!" he called. "Nels, wake up! It's after nine o'clock. I just can't get used to all the darkness. Wake up, you're late for school."

"There is no school today," Nels mumbled from the covers of his bed.

"What do you mean, there's no school today? Why wouldn't there be?"

Nels giggled. "Because it's Saturday," he said. "And even in Alaska, you don't go to school on Saturday."

"Oh. Oh, well, it's a good thing we overslept on a Saturday. Maybe by Monday we'll be used to it. What do you say we go downstairs and eat breakfast?"

"I bet they don't have any Froot Loops," Nels complained.

"Oh, now, what a shame. You might have to eat a real breakfast," Galen said.

*   *   *

After breakfast, Galen went outside to look at the snowmobile that had been provided for him. He leaned down to have a closer examination.

"Good morning," a female voice called.

When Galen looked up, he saw Ellie Springer. She had a small white dog on a leash.

"Good morning, Miss Springer."

"Ellie," she replied.

"Ellie, is it? Well, given how you feel about my being here, I didn't want to presume. I'm Galen."

"Just because I don't approve of what you are doing doesn't mean we can't be cordial," Ellie said.

"I was surprised that you didn't make any comment at the meeting last night."

"Oh, I don't feel that it is my place to comment," Ellie said. "I have my own opinion, as you know. But in the final analysis it's the people who have to decide. I will only teach here for a few more years, at most. They will spend their entire lives here. They are the ones who will have to live with the results of your action."

"Yes, well, I'm glad you're taking that attitude. With the hostility I encountered last night, had you joined in on the other side, I'm afraid I would have been ridden out of town on a rail." Galen's remark was ameliorated by a large grin.

Ellie laughed. "Oh, I don't think it's as bad as all that. You had as many, if not more, supporters as you did adversaries last night."

"They sure didn't say much."

"Why should they? They've got the upper edge right now," Ellie replied. "You're here."

"Yeah, I guess you're right. I hadn't thought about that."

The dog barked.

"Well, now, and who would this be?" Galen looked at the dog, which was gazing at him with a curious expression on its face.

"This is Lady Margaret of Prestonshire, Dowager of Davencourt, Dame of the Tundra," Ellie said. "But, in a pinch, she'll answer to Maggie."

"Whoa. That's quite a long name for such a small dog."

"I got her at the pound, just before I left Dallas," Ellie explained. "And I don't want her intimidated by her humble origins, so I gave her a high-toned name."

Galen laughed, then leaned down to pat Maggie on the head. "It's high-toned all right, but Maggie is enough name for her. You have a fine name, Maggie," he said to the dog. "My mother's name is Maggie, and I think that is noble enough all by itself."

Maggie began licking Galen's hand.

"She likes you."

"Oh yeah, dogs, cats, chickens even. They all like me. It's women I have a hard time with."

Ellie giggled. "Now, I find that hard to believe."

A couple of snowmobiles passed them, the engines roaring loudly. The occupants waved at Ellie, and she returned their waves.

"I guess you know about everyone in town," Galen said.

"Pretty much," Ellie agreed. "That was John Oktollik and Peter Nashookpuk."

"Nash . . . ," he stumbled over the name.

"Nash-ook-puk," Ellie said, phonetically.

"Nashooppuk," Galen repeated, coming closer this time. "I met him last night at the town meeting, I believe."

"Yes, he was up on the stage with you. He's a member of the village council."

"And the other you said was Oktollik?"

"John Oktollik. He's our local radio announcer."

"I didn't know you even had a radio station."

"Oh, yes. Right now he's on a big push to get everyone to get their Christmas shopping done early."

"Christmas shopping—in Point Hope?" Galen laughed. "Excuse me, but it's not like you have a Deerberg's up here. What kind of Christmas shopping could you do?"

"We're remote, yes, but we aren't exactly cut off from the rest of the world," Ellie said. "We can shop on the Internet, we have satellite TV, complete with the shopping channels, and if all else fails, we've still got catalogues. But, because we are remote, we have to get our shopping done early in order for it to be here by Christmas. What about you?"

"What about me?"

"Did you get your Christmas shopping done before you left Dallas? Because it probably would have been smart to do it there."

"No," Galen said. "Nels and I aren't very much into Christmas."

"What do you mean, you aren't 'into Christmas'? Do you mean you don't celebrate it?"

"That's what I mean."

"Why is that?"

"My job keeps me on the go all the time. Keeps us on the go, I should say, since wherever I go, Nels goes as well. It's not always convenient to celebrate Christmas. Especially when you're in countries like Saudi Arabia, which outlaws the celebration of Christmas."

"Oh, I think that's terrible. Didn't Nels miss it? Christmas, I mean."

"You can't miss what you've never had," Galen explained.

"So, what you're saying is that you didn't celebrate Christmas even before you were in Saudi Arabia?"

"That's right."

"Well, it's certainly not my place to interfere. But it seems a shame to deprive a child of Christmas."

"I'm doing him a favor. Whatever meaning Christmas may have had has been so terribly diluted by commercialization now, anyway."

"I'm sorry to hear you say that," Ellie said. "I'm sure the Christmas Festival Committee was counting on some help from you."

"Sorry to disappoint them, but I'm going to be pretty busy over the next several weeks, I'm afraid. That is, if I can figure out how to operate this machine." He turned his attention back to the snowmobile.

"Would you like me to take you for a spin on it, to show you the ropes?" Ellie offered.

"Would you?"

"Sure, I'd be happy to."

"Well, yes, I would like that. I would like that very much."

"Okay, let me get Maggie home before her nose freezes. I'll be back in a few minutes."

"Thanks. I'll be waiting just inside," Galen said, indicating the bed and breakfast.

Galen watched Ellie as she walked away. She had been friendly enough, despite the fact that she was opposed to his being here. And a pretty woman. He laughed. He would have to rely on what he remembered from yesterday, as to how pretty she was. He certainly couldn't tell anything from the bulky parka and winter clothing she was wearing now.

As soon as Galen stepped back into the bed and breakfast, he was met by Molly, who handed him a cup of coffee.

"I saw you looking at the snowmobile. Have you ridden one before?"

"No, I never have. But Miss Springer is going to come back by and check me out on it."

"Really?"

"Yes."

"That is very good. I'm glad to see that Ellie has finally found a boyfriend," she said.

"I beg your pardon?" Galen asked in surprise.

"Well, she's such a pretty young woman. And here she is, up here with nobody to be her boyfriend. It's good to see the two of you courting like that."

Galen chuckled, then took a swallow of his coffee. "We were just talking," he said. "I don't see how you can make that into"—he paused for a moment, then emphasized the word—*"courting."*

"Well, all romances have to start somewhere," Molly said. "I know about these things, you know. I read about it all the time."

"So I see," Galen said, nodding toward the stack of paperback novels in the corner.

"You should read some of them," Molly said. "It will help you with your courtship."

"Well, if I ever get into a courtship situation, perhaps I'll take you up on it," Galen said. "But I assure you, there's no courting going on between Ellie and me."

"Ellie?" Molly asked, picking up on the first name.

"I mean Miss Springer," Galen said. "Besides, I would be the last one she'd be interested in. She's very much against what I'm doing up here."

"Uh-huh," Molly said with a nod of her head. "That's always the way."

"What is always the way? What are you talking about?"

"You would know if you studied the art of romance the way I do."

"Are you trying to tell me that reading romance novels is studying the art of romance?"

"Yes. You see, when the man and woman meet for the first time, there is always some reason that they don't like each other. She doesn't like some of the things he does, and he thinks she's too unfriendly. Like the way Miss Springer doesn't like your job."

"It's not the same thing," Galen protested.

"Yes, it is. You said yourself, she doesn't like what you are doing. But don't worry. Because before they know it, they always find out that they like each other, so whatever was between them at first doesn't matter. After that, things start going really well. Like her going on the snowmobile with you."

Galen finished his coffee. "You know what I think, Molly?" He set the cup down. "I think you should stop reading those things, and start writing them. You have quite an imagination."

"Oh, but wait," Molly said, continuing the explanation. "I need to warn you that something is going to come between you."

"Something is going to come between us?"

"Yes."

"What?"

"I don't know. It's different in every book. But something always happens that separates the man and woman. And when that happens, why it just seems like they'll never get together again. And it'll be like that with you and Ellie, too."

"Oh, it will, will it?" Galen was chuckling again at Molly's lecture.

"Yes. But don't worry. Whatever it is, it'll all work out, and you two will get together once more. That always happens too. In every book."

"Tell me, Molly, will I find oil out there?"

"No," Molly said. "You won't find any oil."

"Well, too bad Pangaea didn't consult with you before I made the flight up here. You could've saved my company a lot of time and a lot of money."

"You won't find oil, but you will find something much more valuable."

"And what will I find that is more valuable than oil? Wait, don't tell me. Love, right?"

"You will find your soul," Molly said.

"My soul?" Galen asked. He laughed. "Tell me, Molly Kowanna, are you an expert on souls?"

"I wouldn't call myself an expert," Molly replied. "But I know about souls."

"I see. And what do you know about souls?"

"I know that, sometimes, we are separated from our soul, perhaps by a great sadness. And that is bad because the longer we are separated from our soul, the longer that great sadness will stay with us."

"That is an . . . interesting observation," Galen said.

"You have experienced a great sadness in your life, haven't you, Mr. Scobey?"

"Of course I have. Everyone has at one time or another," Galen replied stiffly. Molly was getting a little too close to him now, and the conversation was becoming uncomfortable. Fortunately, at that moment the front door opened and Ellie came in.

"Hello, Ellie. Mr. Scobey says you're going to teach him to ride the snowmobile."

"Not much to it," Ellie said. "I'm just going out with him the first time so he can get the feel of it."

"If you'll wait a moment, I'll put some coffee in a thermos for you," Molly offered.

"Thank you, Molly. That would be very nice."

A moment later, carrying the thermos of coffee, Galen and Ellie went back outside to the snowmobile.

"Have you ever ridden a snowmobile before?" Ellie asked.

"No. But I've ridden a motorcycle."

"Well, about the only similarity between this thing and a motorcycle is in the throttle and brake setup. But if you can ride a motorcycle, I'm certain you won't have any trouble with this."

"It is a pretty thing," Galen said as he examined it more closely. "Nice shade of blue."

"This is a Ski-Doo, Grand Touring Five Hundred," Ellie said. "It's made for two riders. Not all of them are. Get on. I'll get on behind you."

"What do you mean? Aren't you going to drive?"

"I'm not the one getting checked out here," Ellie said. "I've already driven one."

Galen began looking around. "Where is the kick starter?" he asked.

Ellie giggled, then reached over and turned a key in the ignition. The engine started.

"Throttle, brake, shift," she said, pointing them out. "It has only two speeds. Forward and reverse. Get on."

Galen got onto the machine, lifted his feet onto the rests, and waited as Ellie climbed on behind him.

"Where to, m'lady?" Galen asked, teasing.

"I'll take you to see Nanny's house."

"Nanny's house?"

"It's about fifteen miles from here," Ellie said. "Nobody lives there now, but for many years an old woman lived there, all by herself. She had to be one of the most isolated people in the world, but it didn't seem to bother her."

"Is there a road to her place?"

"Road? Road? We don' need no stinkin' road," Ellie said, affecting a thick accent.

Laughing, Galen twisted the throttle and the snowmobile leapt forward.

"This is a house?" Galen asked as he and Ellie gazed at the snow-covered mound.

"Yes. It's made primarily of sod." Ellie stepped in through the black maw that was the opening and Galen went with her. He was surprised when she flicked on a flashlight.

"That's a good idea, carrying a flashlight with you," Galen said.

"This time of year I never leave home without it." Ellie played the beam around the inside of the hut. There was only the one room, and the floor, like the walls, was made of mud. There was a circle of stones in the center of the floor, and a hole in the roof.

"And someone lived here?"

"Mary Napakiak lived here for over eighty years. But everyone called her Nanny."

"Eighty years?"

"Yes."

"Wow. If that's the case, this could be nearly a hundred years old."

"This building is older than the United States itself," Ellie said.

"Really? Hard to imagine something that old up here."

"Is it? Let me show you something. I'll drive."

They climbed onto the snowmobile again for a short ride across the tundra. When they stopped, Ellie pointed to several small mounds in the snow.

"This is where the Tikigaq people lived," she said.

"Tikigaq? That's the name of your school."

"Yes. That was the name of the people who lived here then."

"When was that?" Galen asked.

"We are about to celebrate the birth of Jesus," Ellie said. "Three thousand years before the shepherds left the fields to pay their respects to the Christ Child, people were living here."

"Three thousand years BC? You're talking five thousand years?" Galen asked incredulously.

"Yes."

As Galen looked out over the area, he saw four rows of small mounds. They seemed to go on forever.

"How many of these old houses are there?"

"One hundred and fifty," Ellie replied.

"Wow. Have they done any archeological expeditions here?"

"They began digging in 1939, but stopped in early 1942, when the war started. They have done nothing since then."

"Someone should come back up here and do some exploring," Galen said. He saw something protruding from the snow and leaning over, picked it up. Seeing that it was a bone, he tossed it back down.

Ellie laughed. "Don't worry, no human remains here," she said. "Christian missionaries buried them all in the early part of the twentieth century."

"What kind of bone was it?"

"Walrus, probably. Could be whale. It was probably someone's meal."

"Yeah. I wonder when."

"About the time Hannibal was crossing the Alps, perhaps," Ellie suggested.

"I had no idea civilization was that old up here. I'll bet most people don't."

"Archeologists say this is the longest inhabited area on the North American continent. And the thing is, up until the early fifties, you could've taken someone from a thousand years ago and dropped them in the middle of Point Hope and they would scarcely have noticed a difference. I mean, you talk to some of the older people and they can tell you exactly when they saw electricity for the first time, a car, a telephone."

"From what I've seen, you could just about drop one of them in now and they wouldn't be too shocked."

"Oh, that's not true," Ellie said. "Now the people of Point Hope are used to electricity, water, television, telephone. Why, Point Hope may as well be Plano, Texas."

"I know Plano, Texas. I have friends in Plano. I have been to Plano. Point Hope, Miss Springer, is no Plano, Texas."

Ellie laughed at Galen's impersonation of Senator Lloyd Bentsen chiding Dan Quayle.

"We'd better start back," Ellie said. "It is going to be dark very soon."

"Do you ever get used to its being so dark all the time?" Galen asked as they remounted the snowmobile.

"The winter is better than the summer. The dark is easier to adjust to than daylight all the time," Ellie told him.

"Hey, Dad, is Miss Springer your girlfriend?" Nels asked over supper that evening.

"What?"

" 'Cause if she is, I think it would be neat. I mean, she couldn't give me any bad grades if she was your girlfriend, could she?"

"Have you been listening to Mrs. Kowanna?" Galen asked.

"Well, she said . . . "

"I know what she said. No, Miss Springer is not my girlfriend. Besides, since when have you needed help with your grades? You've always made very good grades in school."

"I know. But it would be good not to have to study, especially since I have to be in a play."

"You're going to be in a play?"

"Yes."

"Well, how about that?" Galen said, reaching over to run his hand through Nels's hair. "So, do I have a budding Lionel Barrymore on my hands?"

"Who?"

"Marlon Brando?"

"Who is Marlon Brando?"

"He is a . . . Never mind," Galen said. "Who is some movie actor whose name you do recognize?"

"Josh Hartnett."

"Josh Hartnett," Galen replied. He held his fork in front of his mouth as if it were a microphone.

"And here we are, ladies and gentlemen, standing in front of the theater waiting for the stars to arrive and here is Josh Hartnett. Wait a minute—nobody is going to see him. They are all going over to . . . who is it? Why, yes, it's Nels Scobey. Nels Scobey, ladies and gentle-men, the superduper, double-watusi movie star who got his acting start up in Point Hope, Alaska."

Nels laughed at his father's antics.

~ Seven ~

When Galen and Nels came down to breakfast Monday morning, a small, thin, wrinkled man was sitting at one of the tables, drinking a cup of coffee.

"Your breakfast is coming right up," Molly promised, pouring a cup of coffee for Galen.

"Thanks."

"And for you, young man, hot chocolate," Molly said. "Of course, it's made from powdered milk, but it's pretty good, once you get used to it."

"Everything up here is powdered," Nels said. "Milk, eggs. I'll bet even if we had Froot Loops, they would be powdered."

"Nels," Galen scolded.

"I'm not complaining, Dad," Nels said. "I'm just making an observation."

Galen laughed. "An observation, huh? Well, here's my observation. You'll eat what Mrs. Kowanna puts on the table and be grateful for it."

"I will," Nels promised.

Molly returned with two plates of pancakes.

"Oh, yes," Nels said. "I can be really grateful about this."

"That man over there is Amos Hale," Molly said as she poured the syrup over the pancakes. She nodded toward the smallish man at the other table. "He's here to see you."

"Amos Hale?"

"Mark's father."

"Oh, yes. My guide," Galen said. Turning in his seat, he looked across the room at the only other occupant. "Mr. Hale. Won't you join my son and me?"

Amos got up and crossed over to Galen's table, bringing his coffee with him.

"Mark said you would be needing a guide," Amos said.

"Yes."

"You're looking for oil out in the tundra?"

"Yes, I am."

Amos took a swallow of his coffee and studied Galen for a moment over the rim of the cup.

"Do we need to find anything for me to get paid?"

"No. The pay is the same, whether we find anything or not."

"That's good," Amos said.

"How do you feel about it?" Nels asked.

"How do I feel about what?"

"About developing an oil field here?"

"I don't feel anything about it."

"But surely you have an opinion one way or the other. You're either for it or against it," Galen said.

"I don't need an opinion, because we ain't goin' to find it," Amos said flatly. "That's why I asked if I would get paid even if you didn't find anything."

"How can you be sure we won't find anything?"

Amos put his hand alongside his nose. "I been all over out there. Probably more'n any other man alive. And I know you ain't goin' to find nothin', 'cause I ain't never smelled it."

"You haven't smelled it?"

"Nope."

Galen chuckled. "Well, if it was right on the surface, you might smell it. But if it's two or three miles underground, you wouldn't smell it."

"Yes, I would," Amos replied resolutely.

Galen didn't know what to say. He didn't want to openly challenge Amos, because he did need a guide. "Well, Mr. Hale, that's very remarkable. You'll be quite an asset to me, I'm sure."

"When do we start?"

"We haven't discussed your price."

"You pay? Or big oil company pays?"

"I have an expense account," Galen said. "I'll pay, though ultimately it comes from Pangaea Oil."

"One hundred dollars per day, and gasoline for my snowmobile."

"Snowmobile? I thought you did everything by dogsled."

"For dogsled, two hundred dollars per day," Amos said.

Galen laughed, and held up his hand. "Snowmobile will be fine," he said.

As Ellie Springer's fourth grade prepared for their part in the Christmas play, Rex Hale held up the robe he was to wear as Joseph. "Oh, yuk, why do we have to wear dresses?" he asked.

"Because everybody wore dresses then," one of the other children said. "Even the men."

"Then they were all sissies," Rex insisted.

"Some men over in the Arab countries still wear dresses. I've seen them on TV."

"They aren't dresses," Nels said.

"They are so. I've seen them."

"They aren't dresses," Nels said again. "They are *dishadasha*."

"*Dishadasha,*" Rex said, laughing. "You made that up."

"No," Nels said. He pointed to the robe. "This is the *dishadasha*." He pointed to the headdress. "This is the *shora,* and the black thing that holds it on your head is called an *egal*."

"What do the girls wear?" one of the girls asked.

"The long black veil that the women wear is called a *burqa,*" Nels explained. "The dress they wear is called a *jilbab*."

"How do you know all of that, Nels?" Ellie asked, fascinated by the ease with which Nels was imparting so much information.

"Dad and I were in Saudi Arabia last year," Nels answered.

"That's fascinating. And thank you for sharing it with us. Now, children, everyone take your places. Joey, we don't have your donkey costume finished yet, but if you would get down on your hands and knees anyway, Daisy can ride into Bethlehem on your back."

Ellie had chosen the largest boy in the class to be the donkey, and the smallest and lightest girl to be Mary.

"Now, Nels, you are the narrator. You may begin."

"That's not fair," someone said. "Nels gets to read his part, so he doesn't have to memorize a whole bunch of stuff like we do."

"The reason Nels is reading is because his part is supposed to be read. Also he is our best reader. Besides his part is much, much too long for anyone to memorize."

With everyone in place, Nels began to read: *"And it came to pass in those days, that there went out a decree from Caesar Augustus that all the world should be taxed."*

*   *   *

As Galen and Amos drove their snowmobiles out onto the tundra, each of them pulled a train of sleds behind him. Looking to his left, Galen saw that Amos wasn't sitting, but had climbed up onto the seat and was on his knees. After a while, Galen signaled for them to stop.

The snowmobiles stopped, and the engines were killed. The resulting silence seemed almost crushing. Galen got down, walked to the first of the trailing sleds, and pulled back the tarp, revealing the first of several boxes.

"Help me get this stuff offloaded so I can get it set up," he said.

"Okay."

"Why were you riding like that?"

"Like what?"

"I saw that you were on your knees."

"It's easier to control the machine if you ride on your knees," Amos said, as he began offloading equipment.

The men worked hard for the better part of an hour, getting everything off. Then Galen assembled something that looked like an open pyramid. He also put up a transit scope, as if he were surveying for a highway. He took several readings through the transit scope, then he took a reading from a hand-held global position indicator. After all that was done, he put a few items onto one of the empty sleds, drove several hundred yards, then began doing the same thing all over again.

It was nearly dark by the time he had everything erected.

"What is all this stuff?" Amos asked.

"I'm going to fire explosive charges down into the permafrost, and measure the seismic waves," Galen explained.

"Explosives? You mean like dynamite?"

"Sort of," Galen admitted. "But they are shaped charges, sending the energy down and out through the rocks below. You won't see any surface effect. Okay, step back, I'm ready to shoot."

As George Komack waited at the airport, he glanced again at the magazine article on Clay Berber:

> **Washington, DC**—In a news conference held on the steps of the Environmental Protection Agency and attended by 17 concerned United States Senators and Congressmen, Clay Berber, the activist referred to as the "Civil Defender," expressed utter dismay over recent expansions in the search for new sources of fossil fuel. "The Department of Energy, in concert with the Department of the Interior, has been able to overcome all objections raised by the EPA with regard to destroying our national land heritage in the search for oil," Berber said. "The revelations in several recent news stories confirm our worst fears: This reckless search for oil is completely dismantling decades of EPA guidelines. For the past four years, those of us concerned with our environment have been cautioning the federal government about the grave dangers to our land, water, and ecosystem posed by loosened standards for oil exploration and exploitation. It is now time that the federal government take strong action to protect our environment, and guarantee the heritage of future generations of Americans. We can do this best by looking for new sources of renewable energy rather than the continued rape of our land."

Clay Berber is a well-known activist who often takes
on controversial causes. Before his most recent battle
with the petroleum industry over environmental issues,
he successfully argued to get a display of the Ten Commandments removed from a county courthouse in Mississippi, citing separation of state and religion. He is also a
litigant in a class-action lawsuit against the fast food industry, claiming that their marketing targets the young,
thus contributing to the problem of teenaged obesity.

Seeing Bob Bivens's airplane arrive, Komack put away the magazine, then walked over to the window to watch as the plane taxied up
to the terminal. Shortly after the engines were killed, the cabin door
opened and Berber climbed down from the Twin Beech and strode
quickly across the apron to get inside.

Berber was tall, thin, bespectacled, and gray-haired.

"Mr. Berber?" Komack called.

"Yes. You're Mr. Komack?"

"I am. Welcome to Point Hope." Komack extended his hand.
Berber took it with long, slender fingers, but he kept his hand rather
limp so that, to Komack, it was almost as if he had taken hold of a
fish.

"Thanks for coming," Komack said. "I know we aren't the easiest
place in the world to get to."

"You've got that right," Berber replied in an irritated tone. "I'm
glad to be here, finally. That is one beast of a trip." He turned to point
to the airplane. "And I feel as if I've passed through a time warp.
What is it with that airplane?"

"Oh, that's not so bad. Nearly all of us have ridden *Saigon Sue* at
one time or another," Komack said with a smile.

"I believe you said that the man who is looking for oil is named

Galen Scobey?" Berber said. It was obvious that the small talk was over and he was ready to get down to business.

"Yes. From Pangaea Oil Company. Do you know him?"

"I've never met him," Berber replied, "but I have managed to gather some useful information about him. So, tell me, Mr. Komack, have you managed to secure quarters for me?"

"You'll be staying at the Whalers' Inn," Komack replied. "Come, I'll take you there."

Outside the airport Komack motioned toward a four-wheel, all-terrain vehicle. A rifle and small pack were lashed to the handle-bars.

"You, uh, don't have anything more accommodating?" Berber asked.

"You were expecting a Cadillac?" Komack teased.

"It needn't be a Cadillac."

"Cars and pickups use too much gas," Komack explained. "Up here, every gallon of gas comes in by barge in the summer, and it isn't replenished until the following summer. If we run out, we are out. So it's three dollars a gallon."

Somewhat hesitantly, Berber climbed on behind Komack, then held on as he was driven to a small collection of Atco trailers at the village's western edge.

"I thought we were going to the Whalers' Inn," Berber said.

"This is the Whalers' Inn."

"I see," Berber said. Stiffly, he climbed down from the back of the ATV, then hugged himself. "Well, I don't care where it is as long as it's warm. How can anyone stand to live in this Godforsaken place?"

"Some of us don't consider it Godforsaken," George replied. "That's why we're trying to stop the oil drilling."

"Yes, of course," Berber said. "I was just speaking figuratively."

Although the inn resembled a series of house trailers from the outside, inside they looked like the rooms of any small motel in any town in the lower forty-eight.

"Were you able to locate an office for me?" Berber asked, as he put his luggage on the luggage rack.

George shook his head. "You'll be working out of here," he explained. "Believe me, this is as nice as any place you could find in town."

"Well, like I said, as long as it's warm. What kind of opposition are we facing?" Berber began removing his parka.

"Right now, the majority of the people are in favor of letting Scobey look. Even some of the people who are against drilling."

Berber looked up in surprise. "In favor of letting him poke around out there? Why is that?"

"They say it's because they don't think he's going to find anything, and they believe it would be best to let him search, then go back with a negative report to kill this, once and for all."

Berber shook his head. "Believe me, it doesn't work that way," he said. "Galen Scobey will never submit a report that will completely close the door. Most likely his report will read: 'Requires further exploration.' And that will bring an army of people up here, hell-bent to destroy the ecosystem, all in quest of the almighty dollar. We've got to stop him now."

"Well, how are we going to do that? The Point Hope Village Council and the Tikigaq Corporation have already voted to let him proceed. He also has approval from the North Slope Borough, the state of Alaska, and the Department of the Interior."

"I'll find a way to stop him," Berber said.

~ Eight ~

Galen and Amos went out every day for a week. Each day, Galen set up his equipment, fired off subterranean charges, then took the results from the small seismograph printer. By now, he had several rolls of graph paper, filled with squiggly lines.

The printouts meant nothing to the average person, but with study, Galen would be able to put together a picture of the oil prospects. It was Saturday afternoon, and he had the paper spread out on the small table in his room when there was a knock at the door.

Nels was doing something with some of his new friends, so Galen answered the door himself. It was Molly Kowanna.

"She's here," Molly said.

"Who's here?"

"Her. Your girlfriend."

Galen sighed. "Are you talking about Miss Springer?"

"Yes. She is here."

"She is not my girlfriend."

"Not yet. You're still in what they call the denial stage," Molly said.

Shaking his head, Galen followed Molly into the front parlor.

"Hi," Ellie greeted him. She was holding a file folder. "I thought you might want to see some of Nels's work, to see how he's doing."

"Yes, thank you," Galen said. He reached for the folder. "There's no problem, is there?"

"No, no, he is a wonderful student. And he's done and seen so many things that the rest of my children can only read about. I've been encouraging him to share some of his experiences with us."

Galen chuckled. "He's a talker. You may be opening Pandora's box. Uh, listen, Miss Springer, would you like to have supper somewhere? That is, if there's anywhere in town you could go out to have supper."

"We could go to the Whaler's Café," Ellie suggested. "Or, if that doesn't suit you, we could always go to the Whaler's Café."

It took Galen a second to realize that this was her way of telling him there was only one café in town.

"All right," he said. "Why don't we try the Whaler's?"

"But only if you call me Ellie. There are too few of us *nalokmes* up here to be formal."

"*Nalokmes?*" Then, remembering that was what the children called Nels, Galen laughed. "Oh, yes, non-natives, right?"

"Right."

Like nearly every other building in town, the Whaler's Café reflected the upcoming Christmas season. A wreath hung on the door, and green and red bunting decorated the windows. Inside, an artificial Christmas tree stood in one corner, the many-colored lights shining brightly.

A waitress approached the table. Pinned to her blouse was a golden bell, set in a nest of red and green ribbon. She put a menu in front of each of them: *Finest American and Chinese Food.*

"I'll be back after you've had time to look at the menu," the waitress said. "Merry Christmas."

"Merry Christmas to you as well," Ellie replied brightly. Galen just nodded at her.

"Christmas," Galen said, after the waitress walked away. It was only one word, spoken in a way that was neither reproachful nor approving, though Ellie thought she detected a hint of criticism in his voice.

Galen began studying the menu. "What's good here?"

"How about a pizza?"

Galen chuckled. "Let's see, would that come under American or Chinese?"

"Why, American, of course," Ellie told him.

"Okay, pizza it is."

The waitress returned to take their order.

"And a pitcher of beer," Galen added.

The waitress shook her head. "We can't serve beer," she said. "Point Hope is a dry town."

"All right. Coffee."

"Coffee for me as well," Ellie said.

"We don't have coffee today. We have tea."

"Okay, tea."

The waitress brought a little kettle of hot water and poured it into two cups, over teabags. "Now," she said. "What will it be?"

"A large, double-watusi pizza," Galen said.

"Double-watusi?"

"That means everything. Uh, everything but anchovies." He looked across the table at Ellie. "Is that all right with you?"

"Yes, that's fine with me," Ellie said.

"Okay, one large pizza with everything," the waitress said.

Galen turned to Ellie. "You said you wanted to talk about Nels?"

"I did talk about him. I told you he's a wonderful student and is sharing all of his experiences with the class. Remember?"

"Oh, yes."

"Then, right after that, you asked me out on the town."

"Oh, yes, that's right. So, how about it, Miss Springer?"

"Ellie," she corrected.

"Ellie. Shall we paint the town red? Although, with all the Christmas decorations, there's really no need for that, is there? The town is already red. Red and green."

"Do you really dislike Christmas that much?"

"I don't give it that much thought, one way or the other."

Ellie shook her head. "But that's not true. You've gone out of your way to let it be known that you don't enjoy Christmas."

"I'm sorry, I didn't know I was being that obvious. But you are right. I don't enjoy Christmas."

"Christmas is my favorite time of the year up here," Ellie said.

"Why is that? I mean, I can see how Christmas might be your favorite time of the year, but why do you specify, 'up here'?"

"Because everyone—and I do mean everyone—gets into the spirit of it. Point Hope has a long and storied tradition of celebrating Christmas. It's absolutely unlike anything you've ever seen before."

"I'll be the first to admit that the whole town seems to get into it," Galen said. "There are so many Christmas decorations out you could walk on them from one side of the village to the other without your feet ever touching ground."

"I'm curious, Galen. Just what do you have against Christmas? Why do you dislike it so?"

Before Galen could answer, two men came into the café. One was George Komack. Galen didn't recognize the second man.

"I wonder who that is with Komack?" Galen asked.

"My guess would be Clay Berber," Ellie replied, looking toward the two men.

"Clay Berber? Wait a minute. *The* Clay Berber? The wacko who calls himself the Civil Defender?"

"I don't know that I would call him a wacko," Ellie said. "Although he certainly is an activist."

"He's nothing but a publicity hound," Galen said with a snort. "All he needs is a cause and a microphone and camera. And if you supply the microphone and camera, he's not even that particular about the cause."

"Well, I admit he is something of a grandstander. But I do admire some of the things he's done."

"What's he doing here in Point Hope?"

"He's here because you are," Ellie said.

"What do you mean? What does he have to do with me?"

"Some of the people who oppose what you are doing up here, most noticeably George Komack, got him to come up," Ellie said.

"Why?"

"I imagine it was to see if there was any way they could stop you."

"Well, it's too late to stop me now. I've already gotten the go-ahead from everyone who matters."

"Yes, but if they can muster enough public opinion against you, they might be able to force everyone to take a second look at their authorization."

"That's just great," Galen said irritably. "I don't need to be bothered with this." He took a swallow of his tea and stared across the table at Ellie. "You didn't have anything to do with bringing him here, did you?"

Ellie shook her head and held up her hand. "I promise you,

Galen, I had absolutely nothing to do with bringing Mr. Berber here. I admit that I hope you don't find oil out there, but I certainly won't do anything to try and stop you. As I told you before, even though I've been here for a few years now, I consider myself, at best, a long-term visitor. And, as such, I don't feel that I have a right to interfere one way or the other."

"I wish Berber would take that attitude."

Across the room, George Komack said something to Berber and, nodding, Berber came over to Galen's table.

"Mr. Scobey."

"Mr. Berber."

Berber smiled. "I'm glad you recognized me. That will save me the trouble of introducing myself."

"I didn't recognize you," Galen said. "That's how I knew who you are."

"I beg your pardon?" Berber asked, his face reflecting his confusion at the strange comment.

"I wouldn't expect a *nalokme* to understand. It's a Point Hope thing," Galen said pointedly. He was gratified to see Ellie smile as she took a sip of her tea.

"Yes, well, if you know who I am, then I'm sure you can guess why I'm here."

"My guess is, you're here for whatever publicity you can get out of trying to stop me."

"Oh, we're going to do much more than try, Mr. Scobey. We're going to stop you," Berber said.

"You may be able to stop the actual drilling," Galen said. "But there's nothing you can do to stop me from looking. I have all the authorization I need, from the U.S. Department of the Interior all the way down to the Tikigaq Corporation and the village council of Point Hope."

"I'm sure you promised them you would do no environmental damage during the exploratory process."

"That's right."

"And of course, I'm sure you made that same promise to the people of Madang back in 'ninety-three," Berber said.

Galen's eyes narrowed, and his jaw tightened. "Madang?"

"Yes, Madang. Or did you think something like that would just"—Berber made a waving motion with his hand—"go away?"

"The circumstances here aren't the same, Berber, and you know it," Galen said stiffly.

Berber wagged his finger back and forth. "Ah, but they *are* the same. Everyone knows that what happened in New Guinea wasn't your fault. But that's just the point, don't you see? How do you know that something like what happened there—oh, maybe not the same thing, but something completely unforeseen—can't happen here?"

At that moment the waitress arrived with the pizza.

"If you'll excuse us, Berber, our meal is here," Galen said.

"Yes, of course. Enjoy," Berber said before returning to George Komack.

"Do you like crushed red peppers on your pizza?" Galen asked, reaching for them.

"Yes. And you can't put too many for me," Ellie replied.

As Galen doctored the pizza, he noticed, with some appreciation, that Ellie didn't question him about Berber's comment. And, because she didn't question him, he offered to explain.

"I suppose you'd like to know what happened in Madang."

"Only if you want to tell me," she said.

"New Guinea is an oil-producing nation. In 1993, the government of New Guinea signed an agreement with Pangaea Oil to search for new oil fields. I was still pretty new in the business, and that was the first time I was ever site director."

He paused for a moment and took a swallow of tea, as if forming his next sentence. "In order to understand what happened, you have to remember that, during World War II, New Guinea was one of Japan's major forward areas. And, in support of their military operation, they brought in tons of military supplies. In fact, one of the tourist attractions today is an underwater exploration of the Japanese war planes on the bottom of the bay."

Galen toyed with his pizza, but he didn't take a bite.

"I began my search by setting off subterranean explosions, just as I'm doing here, in order to get seismic readings. One of the charges broke through into an underground tunnel system that nobody knew anything about. That tunnel was filled with Japanese ordnance. There was a ripple explosion effect, all along the path of the tunnel. And the tunnel passed right under a native hut . . . " He couldn't continue.

Ellie reached across the table to put her hand on his. Instead of just touching it, she squeezed it, and looked at him with eyes filled with compassion.

"There were, uh"—Galen paused, took a deep breath, and continued—"two people in that hut. An old man and his wife. Both were killed instantly."

"Oh, Galen, I'm so sorry."

"He was seventy-six, she was seventy-two. Do you have any idea how it makes me feel to know that two human beings who had been on earth for most of the twentieth century . . . who had seen their island move from the Stone Age to the modern age, had survived wars, earthquakes, and hurricanes . . . had their lives ended by something that I did?"

"I know it has been difficult for you to live with that," Ellie said. "And you are right, the circumstances are totally different. Berber had no right to even bring it up."

"Perhaps. But he is going to bring it up. And I'm sure it's going to cause some difficulty."

Ellie smiled at him. "Why is it that I believe you aren't a stranger to overcoming difficulty?"

"Our pizza is getting cold," Galen said, anxious to change the subject.

Ellie took a bite. "Oh my, this is very good. Why, we could be eating at Maggiano's Little Italy back in Dallas," she said, speaking of one of Dallas's more upscale Italian restaurants.

Galen had just taken a bite of his own pizza and, laughing out loud, he had to put his hand over his mouth to keep from spewing food.

"I'd say you pretty well nailed it," he said, wiping his lips with his napkin. "Yes, this is just like Maggiano's."

When they walked outside after dinner, Galen was amazed at how light it was.

"I don't understand this," he said. "The sun set a long time ago."

"It's the northern lights," Ellie said. "When they are out and reflecting back from the snow, it's almost bright enough to read by."

"I had no idea it could get this bright."

"It's our little secret," Ellie said. "It's like God is compensating us for the fact that He took the sun away in the winter."

Galen laughed. "So you think God just took a personal interest in the folks up here by hanging a big old electric light bulb in the sky, do you?"

"Do you have a better explanation?"

"What? You want me to explain what the northern lights are? Because I can, you know." Galen smiled. "You picked the wrong subject to challenge me on. It just so happens that I wrote a paper about the northern lights for my science project when I was in high school."

"All right, let me hear your explanation."

Galen cleared his throat, as if about to give a lecture. "The northern lights are the result of the solar wind, which is actually a stream of protons spewed out from the Sun," he said. "When those protons reach Earth, they collide with atoms in our upper atmosphere, loosing electrons. As those electrons are loosed, light is emitted."

"So tell me, Mr. Science Project, what is electricity if it isn't the flow of electrons?" Ellie asked.

"Well, uh . . . ," Galen paused, then chuckled. "All right, I guess you've got me on that one."

"Then God hung an electric light in the sky for us, didn't He?"

"If you believe all things come of God, then, yes. But to say God took a personal interest in the people of Point Hope would be stretching it a bit, don't you think?"

"Are you saying God never takes a personal interest in anyone, or anything?"

"Yeah, that's pretty much what I'm saying." There was a hint of bitterness in Galen's voice.

"You have been hurt, haven't you?"

"Let's don't talk about it anymore."

"All right," Ellie agreed.

Galen smiled, and changed the subject. He pointed to the snowmobile. "Get on," he said. "I'm really getting good with this thing now. I'll take you home."

Ellie climbed on behind Galen and he drove her home. He was halfway there before he realized that he didn't even have the light on, so bright was the aurora borealis display tonight. Pulling up in front of her house, he turned off the ignition. After the roar of the little two-cycle engine, the silence was deafening.

"Would you like to come in, Galen?" Ellie asked, as she climbed off the machine. "I can give you that cup of coffee you didn't get at the restaurant. Along with a piece of carrot cake," she added.

"Carrot cake? Now, you really are a temptress," he said. "Yes, I think I'll take you up on your offer."

Ellie picked up a cord and plugged it into Galen's machine in order to keep the engine warm.

"All right," she said. "Come on in."

Maggie ran to greet them when they stepped inside.

"Hello, Maggie," Galen said, squatting down to pat the little dog as she rolled over on her back, presenting her underside.

"Wow, she's really playing hard to get," Ellie teased as she took off her parka. "Here, I'll hang yours up."

Standing, Galen took off his parka, looking around her house as he did so. "Nice place," he said.

"Thanks. It's a little small."

"Small?" Galen laughed. "Compared to the single room Nels and I are sharing, this is like a palace."

"I guess that was unthinking of me," Ellie said. She pointed to the sofa. "Have a seat. I'll get the coffee and cake."

When she came into the living room a few minutes later carrying a tray with coffee and cake, Galen was sitting on the sofa and Maggie was beside him, her head resting on Galen's leg. Galen was rubbing Maggie behind the ears.

"By the way, disabuse yourself of any idea that you've won Maggie over by your charm," Ellie teased, putting the tray down on the table. "She's a real tramp and will go after any man who pays the slightest bit of attention to her. Cream and sugar?"

"Black, please," Galen said, taking the cup from her.

There was a clicking sound as the thermostat kicked in and the fan pushed a column of warm air from the oil-fired furnace into the room. The warm air felt good.

"I envy you, not only your room but your sofa," Galen said. "I'm a sofa person, but in our room, we have only our beds, a couple of chairs, and a desk."

"Well, please feel free to use my sofa any time you begin to get a real sense of sofa deprivation," Ellie offered. She sat down on the sofa beside him, ostensibly to begin petting Maggie.

"I must say, I didn't expect to find anything like this up here," Galen said.

"What? You mean a house? What did you expect, a bunch of igloos?"

"No, I knew there would be houses up here. That's not what I'm talking about."

"What *are* you talking about?"

"The opportunity for social interaction with an agreeable and attractive . . . *nalokme*," he said, smiling.

Ellie laughed. "You are really getting a lot of use out of that word today, aren't you?"

"It's a good word to know," Galen replied.

They talked for nearly an hour, Ellie describing some of her experiences since coming to Alaska, and Galen some of the remote areas he had been to. The conversation was pleasant and often humorous.

For the entire time, because Ellie was sitting on the couch, separated from him only by Maggie's body, they were very close together. Then slowly, almost imperceptibly, Galen moved his head toward her until their lips were only a breath apart.

As they looked at each other, Ellie knew that she had already crossed the Rubicon. He was going to kiss her, and she was going to allow it. And yet, she knew that she should make one final effort to prevent it.

"Galen, I'm not sure this is . . . ," she started to say, but even as she was talking, their lips met.

It wasn't a probing, demanding kiss. It was a gentle kiss, as soft as the brush of a butterfly's wing, yet its very tenderness evoked an unexpected response from Ellie. She knew at that moment that Galen controlled the situation. She put herself in his hands.

Galen pulled away after a moment.

"I—uh—should get back," he said, as if suddenly finding himself in an uncomfortable situation.

"Are you frightened, Galen Scobey?" Ellie asked.

"Frightened? Of what?"

"Of me. Us. This," she said with an inclusive motion of her hand.

"No, don't be silly. I'm not frightened. Whatever gave you that idea? It's just that . . . well, it's getting late. That's all."

Ellie giggled. "Oh yes, it's late, all right. It's a little after eight."

"Eight?" Galen looked at his watch. "You're right. It is just a little after eight. But I think I'd better get on back anyway." He stood up.

"All right, I'm not going to try to hold you against your will," Ellie said. She stood as well, and walked with him to the front door. "Thank you for the pizza. And I truly did enjoy the evening."

"I did, too," Galen said. "Listen, about what just happened in there. I—uh—" He let the sentence hang, unable to complete his thought.

"Don't worry about it, Galen Scobey. Nothing happened," Ellie said, smiling sweetly at him. "Good night."

"Good night."

Galen put on his parka, then walked out front and mounted his snowmobile. Because it had been connected to an electric engine warmer, it kicked over easily.

He looked back toward Ellie's front door, intending to wave if he saw her at the window, but she wasn't there.

Why had he apologized for what had happened? It certainly wasn't something unpleasant for him, and he was reasonably sure it wasn't unpleasant for her.

I handled it badly, he thought. I'm afraid that right now she thinks I am either a timid wimp or an arrogant idiot.

~ Nine ~

"Maggie, I'm afraid I handled this rather badly," Ellie said, immediately after Galen left.

Maggie stared up at her.

"I mean, after my performance tonight, I'm sure he thinks I'm either an aggressive broad or a shameless hussy."

Maggie put a paw on Ellie's leg.

"You want to go out?"

Maggie ran to the front door, then looked back at her.

"Okay, but wait a moment," Ellie said. "I don't want to take you out until he's gone. After the way I acted tonight, it might look as if I'm chasing after him."

Maggie stared at Ellie with a demanding, unwavering gaze.

"All right, all right, I told you we would go. Just give me just a minute or two, will you?"

Maggie continued to stare.

"Oh, okay, let me look," Ellie said. Pulling the blinds apart, she saw that Galen was well away. She also saw that her neighbor across the street was looking through her blinds.

"Okay, he's gone," Ellie said, reaching for her parka. "Let's go."

Maggie's tail started wagging excitedly as Ellie got ready to take her outside.

Ellie thought of the kiss she had just shared with Galen. Of course, she had told him that nothing happened, but clearly something had. Although she could not say that the kiss had been particularly passionate, it was a lot more than a friendly peck. It was clearly a kiss that promised more. The question was . . . what, exactly did it promise? And, did she want more?

Ellie's experience with men was rather limited. She had dated Kevin Bollinger, a law student at SMU, during her last two years of college. It had been a pleasant association, though not a passionate one. Kevin was a convenience, always there when she needed an escort. But she knew, well into their relationship, that he wasn't the one she would wind up with.

When Ellie left Dallas, Kevin took her to the airport and waited with her until she had to go to the boarding gate. It was not difficult to tell him good-bye. In fact, she welcomed it as a way of finally terminating the relationship.

Ellie suspected that Kevin felt the same sense of relief, and that suspicion was borne out a year later when he sent her a friendly letter. He was now practicing law in San Francisco and was about to get married.

Ellie realized that, in coming to Alaska, she would be putting on hold any opportunity for romance. And that was exactly the way things turned out. The first year she was here, she had gone to dinner a few times with the basketball coach. But that had been the last year of his teaching contract and he didn't renew it. The next year she had dinner with a visiting college professor. Tonight was her first date in over a year.

Ellie had known before taking the job, had been warned by the recruiters, that there would be very little social life for her. But she had accepted that, believing that the sacrifice of any personal life was worth the return she would realize in adventure and experience.

Her other social opportunities, with the basketball coach and the visiting professor, had been just that—social opportunities.

Then Galen Scobey came to Point Hope.

Galen was good-looking, interesting, and available. And she had to admit that she had enjoyed the evening she spent with him. In fact, she let herself enjoy it more than she thought she would, because she considered him a safe diversion. After all, he wasn't going to be here long enough for anything to get serious. Besides, he had a son, and that, too, would keep things from going too far. It wasn't like she wanted a ready-made family or anything.

Maggie moved through the snow, sniffing here, then there, until she found just the right place. As Maggie squatted, Ellie looked toward Kay Nagotchak's window and, seeing that the blinds were still parted, she waved. The blinds closed immediately.

"Oh, Kay, Kay, don't you think I know you've been staring across the street all night?" Ellie said under her breath. She giggled. "In fact, you've been staring across the street for the last three years."

Kay Nagotchak was a seventy-six-year-old widow. Until fairly recently, Point Hope had been so isolated that there was neither television, radio, nor telephone. With the introduction of communications satellites, all three became available, but the phone service was the most welcome to Kay.

Despite being denied the use of the telephone for most of her life, it took Kay, an inveterate gossip, no time at all to master the instrument. As a result, Ellie knew that by tomorrow everyone in town would know that she had been out with Galen tonight, just as they had known about each date she had with the basketball coach, and with the visiting college professor.

Finished with her business, Maggie started back toward the front door, pulling so hard against the leash that her feet were slipping on the snow.

"Don't be so impatient, I'm hurrying, I'm hurrying," Ellie protested as she followed along behind the little dog.

Molly Kowanna was sitting in the parlor when Galen returned. Looking up at him, she smiled broadly.

"How was your date with Miss Springer?"

"Date? Oh, well, it wasn't really what I would call a date."

"Did you take her to dinner?"

"Yes. We had a pizza at the Whaler's."

"You went home with her."

"I took her home, yes."

"And you went in the house with her."

"I—how do you know I went into the house with her?"

"Kay Nagotchak told me."

"Kay Nagotchak?"

"She is my friend. She lives across from Miss Springer. She heard you bring her home, and when she looked through the window, she saw you go inside with her. You were there for nearly an hour."

"She timed how long I was there?"

"With a stopwatch." Molly pointed to her wrist. "She has a watch like the one they use to time runners. She punches a button and it starts, and she punches another button and it stops. You were there for fifty-seven minutes and twenty-three seconds," Molly said with a broad grin.

"She timed me with a stopwatch? Isn't there a satellite TV show Kay Nagotchak could be watching?"

"Did you kiss her?"

"Well, I don't know. What did Kay Nagotchak tell you about that?"

"She couldn't see when you went inside."

"Well, thank God for that!"

"Did you kiss her?"

"Molly, you are entirely too interested in my love life."

Molly squealed with delight and clapped her hands together. "You see, it *is* your love life. I knew it would be this way. It has gone to the next step now, just like it does in all the books."

"There *is* no next step," Galen said in exasperation.

"Sure there is." The smile left Molly's face and she held up her finger with a look of concern on her face. "But, don't forget, after this, something bad will happen and it will drive you apart. And when it does, you will think that nothing can bring you together again."

"Molly, will you quit with this already? I am not going to play out a romance novel for you. Can't you find something else to read? How about science fiction?"

Molly shook her head. "Science fiction isn't real."

"Neither is this."

"When I asked if you kissed her, you didn't answer," Molly said.

"No, and I'm not going to answer. I simply am not going to talk about this with you."

"Why not?"

"Because there are some things I would just as well keep to myself."

"This is a small village. There are no secrets in Tikigaq."

"So I'm beginning to find out," Galen said drily. "Okay, I'm going to my room now." He looked at his watch. "This isn't a stopwatch, so I have no idea how long we have been talking. But I can tell you that it is ten minutes until nine. I suggest you call Kay Nagotchak and tell her. I wouldn't want her to have to spend the rest of the night looking through her front window, trying to see what was going on."

Molly smiled. "She knows that you're back. She called to tell me. Now I will call her and tell her that you kissed Miss Springer good night."

"*What?* What makes you think that? If you recall, I didn't answer your question."

"Not with words," Molly said. "But here." She put her fingers to her own lips. "You answered it here."

"And just how did I do that?"

"You have lipstick here, I think."

Quickly, Galen put his hand to his mouth and began wiping. Molly's laughter followed him all the way back to his room.

"Hi, Dad," Nels said, looking up from the TV. "How was your date with Miss Springer?"

"It was fine," Galen said in exasperation. "It was just fine."

"Good," Nels replied without asking for any more details. Turning his attention back to the TV program, he laughed.

"Turn it down just a little, would you, Nels?" Galen asked, thankful that Nels didn't press the issue. "I want to look at these readouts."

"Okay, Dad."

Galen lay back on his bed and held the pages up, examining the squiggly lines on the printouts from today's tests. So far, he had seen no significant patterns emerging. The results were interesting without being especially promising. At this point he couldn't recommend that they start test drilling; but neither could he advise that they would be wasting their time to do so.

Often, the type of testing he was doing would yield very clear results, either a strong indication of oil or an even clearer indication that there was nothing below. The readings he was getting this time were inconclusive in that some tests were promising while others were not.

It was results like these that made his job hard, because ultimately it would depend upon his interpretation. And that interpretation sometimes crossed over into guesswork. Galen would hate to admit it, but with the readings he was getting now, Amos Hale's insistence that there was no oil because he couldn't smell it was just as likely to be accurate as these high-tech observations.

He studied these and his earlier reports, trying to see if he could make any sense out of them. At some point after ten, Nels turned off the TV and crawled into his own bed. Galen continued to study until his eyes grew heavy. A couple of times he jerked them open, realizing with some surprise that he had actually been asleep.

"Nels, maybe you'd better—" Galen started, then he interrupted himself. He was going to tell Nels it was time to turn off the TV and go to bed, but Nels had already done that. Galen had been so involved with the printouts that he hadn't even noticed. Reaching over to the bedside lamp, he turned it off; then, taking off his clothes, he slipped under the cover. He was asleep within moments.

A part of Galen was aware that he was dreaming. And yet the dream was so detailed in its construction, and so intense in the emotion it engendered, that against all reason, Galen was ready to accept it as reality. It did not seem at all strange to him that his wife, who had been dead for seven years, was with him.

"More decorations?" Galen asked, as Julia came into the house carrying packages of lights, ornaments, and tinsel. "What are you trying to do? Turn us into Christmas wonderland?"

"All of this is for Nels," Julia said. "He was too young to celebrate Christmas last year."

Galen laughed. "He's only two years old now. I think you're just using him as an excuse."

"Maybe, but he does enjoy all the decorations. Why, you should see his little face shine when I light up the Christmas tree."

"Ha! It's not shining, it's reflecting. You've got more lights on that tree than the White House Christmas tree."

"Exaggeration does not become you, Galen Scobey," Julia said. She pulled a little green and red jumpsuit from a sack. "Now, what do you think of this? Isn't it just the cutest, most adorable thing you ever did see?"

"What is it?"

"It's a Santa's elf costume for Nels."

"It's sort of a waste to buy something like that, isn't it? I mean, he can only wear it for Christmas, and by the time Christmas comes around again next year, he'll have outgrown it."

"Oh, don't be such a Grinch," Julia teased. "At his age he needs new clothes about every few months anyway, so we may as well get him something that's fun."

"Fun, huh?" Galen snorted.

"Yes, I think he'll have loads of fun with it," Julia insisted.

"Are you kidding? At his age he wouldn't know the difference between an elf suit and a gunnysack with holes cut in it," Galen said resolutely.

"Shows how much you know about children," Julia said. She reached for one of the boxes from her Christmas shopping spree. "Oh, here. I want you to see this." Opening the box, Julia took out a rather large glass star that had its own light. She plugged it in to demonstrate. The glass had several angles and facets, beveled in such a way that it greatly increased the brightness of the light.

"Whoa!" Galen said, putting his hands over his eyes. "If you put this *on the tree, the only way we'll be able to look at it is by staring through one of those little pinholes like you use to watch a solar eclipse."*

Julia laughed. "Oh, pooh. I think it's beautiful. Will you put it on the top of the tree for me?"

"All right, I'll put it up there. But don't blame me if three strange-looking bearded dudes wearing long robes and riding camels show up on our front porch bearing gifts of gold, frankincense, and myrrh."

Julia clapped lightly. "Why, Galen, I'm impressed. I didn't know that you knew even that much of the Bible."

"Like this cut-glass star, my dear, I am a man of many facets," Galen said. He climbed onto a chair and began fixing the ornament.

As he did so, Nels wandered into the living room, rubbing his eyes.

"Nels, what are you doing out of bed? I thought we had put you down for the night?"

"Drink," Nels said, only the word came out as "dink."

"You want a drink, huh? Okay, I'll get you some water," Julia said. She picked the little boy up and held him, then pointed to the top of the tree. "But first, I want you to look at what Daddy is doing."

"Daddy is creating an aviation hazard, that's what Daddy is doing," Galen said from the chair. He was reaching over his head, and his arms were thrust elbow-deep into the green boughs. "When we turn this thing on, they'll have to reroute all the traffic into DFW because of the light.

"Okay, I've got it." He climbed down from the chair and looked back up for a last check of his work.

Julia was still holding Nels. "Galen, turn all the room lights off, would you? Then turn the Christmas tree on," she said. "I want Nels to see it."

"Okay. But are you sure you want to do this without sunglasses?"

Julia laughed. "Just do it."

Galen turned off all the room lights, then he plugged in the Christmas tree and turned on the glass star at the top. The star was exceptionally bright, but not so bright as to diminish the effect of the multicolored lights. Even Galen had to admit it made quite an effective display.

"Oh, look at that, Nels!" Julia said. "Isn't it beautiful?"

The star was glowing so brightly that it radiated brilliant bars of light from its center, giving the effect of extending each of its five arms.

Nels smiled broadly and pointed to the star. He laughed out loud. "Mama!" he said. "Mama!"

"See? I told you he would like it," Julia said, giving Nels a hug and a kiss. "Come along, now, sweetie. I'll get you some water, then it's back to bed with you."

Galen stayed in the living room, just looking at the tree, until Julia returned.

"Did you get him put down all right?"

"I did." She stood next to him and Galen put an arm around her, then pulled her closer. "Now, you have to admit, that is beautiful," Julia said.

"It is," Galen said. "But not as beautiful as you are."

Smiling up at him, Julia turned toward him to kiss him, and Galen felt her lips on his.

But it wasn't Julia who kissed him. It was Ellie. Galen jerked back . . . then awoke with a start.

— Ten —

George Komack managed to get another town meeting called in order to hear a few words from Clay Berber. It was not an official meeting; no decision could or would be made that would change the situation with regard to Galen's exploratory operation. But it could have an effect on the villagers' attitude; and, as Ellie pointed out, it would probably be good for Galen to be there.

"I thought you were against what I'm doing," Galen said.

"I am against it in principle," Ellie replied. "I would not like to see Point Hope changed. But if you weren't here, someone else would be." She smiled. "And, as they say, the devil you know is preferable to the devil you don't know."

Galen laughed out loud. "Thanks . . . I think."

As before, the meeting was held in the school gymnasium. This time, though, Galen was not sitting on the stage but out in the auditorium with the others. George Komack and Clay Berber were on stage, and they were the only two there. Their chairs were at stage right, with the speaker's podium in the middle; a large projection screen stood at stage left.

As Galen waited for the meeting to begin, he looked around the gym and saw that the Christmas decorations were even more abundant than they had been at the previous meeting. Now, in addition to the greenery, lights, and Christmas trees, the walls were decorated with pictures, obviously drawn by the students. The quality of the drawings ranged from the crude efforts of the younger grades to a few very good pictures by the older students.

The gym filled up quickly as the villagers came in; here and there, Galen heard snatches of conversation in the native language. He leaned over toward Ellie, who was sitting beside him.

"Do you understand what they're saying?"

Ellie shook her head. "No. But if you are in their presence, they are pretty good about either speaking English or letting you in on what they are talking about."

The room buzzed with a hundred or more separate conversations until George Komack stepped up to the podium. He stood there for a moment, making no effort to silence anyone, just looking out over the crowd. One by one, as people saw him standing there, they stopped their conversation. Finally, the entire auditorium grew quiet.

"I want to thank all of you for coming tonight," he began.

"Why are we here, George?" someone called from the audience. "We've already decided to let them look for oil. What are you trying to do? Mess it up for everyone?"

The challenge was answered with several voices who agreed with the questioner, but also with several voices who let it be known that they wanted a little more discussion on the subject.

"Let's hear what he has to say," one of the others called.

"Thank you," Komack said. He cleared his throat. "As all of you know, I am against drilling for any oil up here. Not only am I against drilling for it, I am against looking for it. I've made no secret about this. I have felt this way from the beginning. I think the people of Point Hope were"—he waved his hand back and forth in front of his eyes—"dazzled by the promise of how much money they could make."

"What's wrong with making money, George?" someone shouted, and the others laughed.

"I'll tell you what is wrong with it," Komack replied. "What is wrong with it is, you were thinking only about the money, and not about what could happen if we just plunged head-on into this. So, I've brought someone up here to speak to us about some of the things we might want to consider. Some of you have heard of him, because he has been very outspoken on environmental issues for many years. Ladies and gentlemen, our guest speaker tonight is the famous Civil Defender, Clay Berber."

There was a polite round of applause as Berber stepped up to the podium.

"Would you dim the lights please?" Berber asked.

The lights were dimmed and Berber clicked a remote-control device. On the screen there appeared the picture of what was obviously a very heavy sheen of oil on the surface of the sea.

"Valdez, March 24, 1989," Berber began. "A drunken ship's captain drove his ship onto the rocks. The ship was carrying fifty-three million gallons of crude oil. The tanks ruptured, and before they could get the spill contained, eleven million gallons of black, poisonous oil spewed out into the sea."

There were several oohs and ahhs from the audience.

"Point Hope is one of the very few places in the world where whales may be legally harvested. It is not only your livelihood, it is your sacred heritage. Can you imagine what a foot-thick coating of oil would mean to the whales?"

He clicked the remote. This time the picture showed a very heavy deposit of oil on the rocks ashore.

"This is what your coastline would look like," he said.

He clicked another picture. It was the same kind of picture, oil sludge on the rocks, but this time a man was bent over, sticking a ruler down into the sludge.

"As you can see, this is not a light covering. It is several inches thick, here."

He clicked, and a new picture came up. "And, as you can see by this picture, the damage was not limited to Valdez Bay alone. This is many miles away, for it spread all along the entire intertidal zone."

He clicked again. "Here it is, all the way to the back of the bay. I'm sure you can understand that if that happened here, the entire Point would be contaminated. If what happened at Valdez happened here, this ancient place we call Point Hope, and you call Tikigaq, would be uninhabitable for the next one thousand years."

That brought a very loud reaction from the audience as they contemplated the idea of losing their home for a millennium.

"I have one last picture to show you," Berber said. He clicked again, and this time the screen displayed several seals, covered in oil.

"In addition to taking whales, you also hunt for seal. You can see, here, what the oil industry would do to your seals. Lights, please."

The lights came back on.

"I know that the decision has already been made to allow oil production to go on up here," Berber continued. "But that decision was made with the understanding that it enjoyed the support of the people who would feel the greatest impact. That means they believe they have your support," he concluded, pointing to the audience. "But that also means that if you were to reconsider your support, I guarantee you, the government would listen . . . and you would not have to face the terrible consequences faced by the people of Valdez."

The audience applauded, and Berber sat down. Komack stood.

"I'm going to call now for a vote from all of you. If we make our voices heard, here in the village council and the Tikigaq Corporation, we can stop this. Our voice will be heard in the North Slope Borough, in Juneau, and in Washington, D.C. We can make certain that what happened at Valdez will never happen to us."

"Hold on a minute, George," Percy Tokomik called from the audience. "I see Mr. Scobey in the audience. Let's hear what he has to say about all this."

Several others backed Tokomik's call to hear from Galen.

"Mr. Scobey, you want to come up here and speak about this?" Komack invited, stepping away from the platform.

"I'd rather not," Galen said.

Komack chuckled. "I didn't think you would." Komack looked back at the audience. "You heard him, folks. He said he'd rather not talk about what Mr. Berber just showed us. And I don't blame him for not wanting to comment. There is nothing he can say to answer these charges. I think it's about time for that unanimous petition to the council and corporation."

"Galen, unless you want to see this thing end right here, you'd better get up there and say something," Ellie cautioned.

Sighing, Galen stood up. "All right," he said. "I'll address his charges."

Tokomik and some of the others showed their support by applauding.

"But I'll just talk from here, if you don't mind." Galen turned to face the others.

"In 1998, Bill Clinton was still president. President Clinton billed himself as a strong supporter of the environment, and there are few who would argue that point with him. He was against any further Alaskan oil development, or even exploration. I tell you all that so that you will know that what I am about to say isn't a whitewash.

"Because you see, in 1998, during the Clinton administration, the EPA authorized a fully funded, in-depth appraisal of the Exxon oil spill, and its impact, ten years later. For those of you with access to the Internet, you can find the results of that examination on line. What it says is that there is 'little measurable impact,' ten years after the event. The sea is clear, and the beaches and rocks are clean, partially as a result of a cleanup process, but more as the result of nature. In fact, most scientists agree that even if we had done nothing at the time of the spill, today the impact would still be minimal.

"Four species of wildlife were investigated: the harbor seals, pink salmon, several of the seabirds, and otter. The result of that examination was that the wildlife suffered no negative impact.

"I won't lie to you—the spill was a terrible thing. But it was the result of a preventable human accident, not an intrinsic result of the production of oil. What that means is, just because it happened at Valdez, that is no sign that it would happen here. Mr. Berber would have you believe that such spills are the inevitable result of oil exploration and production. That simply isn't true. Valdez was not only human error, it was egregious human error, the result of one man's criminal incompetence."

Galen sat down to applause; before it ended, Berber was back at the podium.

"I don't disagree with you that it was an accident. And in this case, it was preventable because the captain was drunk. But what about those accidents that happen to the most careful of men? Doesn't that just prove that accidents are inevitable?"

"Not necessarily," Galen replied.

"I see. Then the accident you had in New Guinea was due to what—your carelessness?"

By now, the story of what had happened at New Guinea had

made the rounds so that, at Berber's mention, everyone in the auditorium gasped.

Galen looked at Ellie in surprise. "You told someone about that?"

Ellie shook her head. "I haven't told anyone," she said. "I didn't have to. No doubt Mr. Komack did, and this is a very small village. I'm sure the story was in every home in the village by midnight last night."

"Well, what about it, Mr. Scobey?" Komack asked. "Can you guarantee that something like that won't happen here?"

"You mean, can I guarantee that I won't set off another hidden cache of Japanese ordnance?" Galen replied. He nodded. "Yes, Mr. Berber. I think I can guarantee that."

The audience laughed and applauded.

"Go ahead and hold your vote if you want to, George," Luke Koonook said. "But I intend to vote exactly as I did before, and I believe the others will as well. As far as I'm concerned, Mr. Scobey can continue his exploration."

Koonook's words were also greeted with applause.

"All right," Komack said, holding up his hands in frustration. "We won't vote now. We'll let Scobey continue to poke around out on the tundra." He pointed his finger at Galen. "But be advised, Mr. Scobey, that I, and others like me, will keep our eyes on you. And at the very first indication that something is going amiss, we will stop you."

Komack's supporters applauded him.

"You won," Ellie said as the meeting broke up.

"For now," Galen replied.

"I have some of that carrot cake left, if you'd like to come over for a piece."

"What if Kay Nagotchak finds out?"

Ellie laughed. "What if she finds out? Why, Galen, she *expects* it."

~ *Eleven* ~

"Dad, do you remember how you said that I probably wouldn't even know that it was Christmas up here?" Nels said over breakfast the next morning.

"Yes, I remember."

"Well, you were wrong."

Galen chuckled. "I'll admit that. I've never seen such a frenzy over Christmas."

"I wondered if you remembered what you said about it."

"Trying to rub it in to the old man, are you?"

"No," Nels said. "Oh, by the way, today we're having the first dress rehearsal for our play. Do you know what a dress rehearsal is?"

"Well, I think I know," Galen replied. He smiled back at Nels. "But you, being in show business, probably understand better than I do. So, suppose you tell me what it is."

Nels put jelly on his biscuit as he began explaining. "It's where everybody puts on their costume, you know, whatever they are going to wear? And we do the whole play, just like we're going to do it Christmas Eve."

Galen was about to take a sip of his coffee, but he put it back down and looked across the table at Nels.

"Christmas Eve? Wait a minute. You're doing this play on Christmas Eve?"

"Sure. That's the best time to do it," Nels said. "I mean, it's a Christmas play, so you should do it on Christmas. Or Christmas Eve."

"I didn't know it was a Christmas play."

"Yep."

"What's the play about?"

"It's about the first Christmas. You know, when Jesus was born? I'm the narrator. That's the best part, because I don't even have to learn any lines."

"What do you mean, you don't have to learn your lines? You're in the play, aren't you?"

"Yes, but my part comes from the Bible. I read the story from the Bible and the others have to act their part out."

"I see," Galen said.

"Miss Springer said the whole town will come to watch the play."

"Oh, I doubt the whole town will turn out."

"Dad, you just don't know how big Christmas is up here. That's all anyone has been talking about, almost ever since we arrived."

"Yes, so I've noticed."

"Dad, I know you don't like Christmas," Nels began. "But . . ."

"It isn't that I don't like Christmas, Nels," Galen interrupted. "It's just that"—he paused for a moment, trying to find the right words—"I thought we both agreed that celebrating Christmas without your mother would be too sad for you."

"I know we've said that," Nels said. "But, Dad, whether we celebrate Christmas or not, everyone else is. And if it's going to make us sad anyway, then we may as well celebrate it too."

"Why, all of a sudden, are you so intent on this? The fact that we don't celebrate Christmas has never bothered you before."

"I know. But last Christmas, and the Christmas before, we were in Saudi Arabia. Nobody celebrates Christmas in Saudi Arabia. And the year before that, we were on a plane flying to South America on Christmas Day, so we didn't celebrate that one either. I've never really been around Christmas until we came up here."

"That's true," Galen admitted.

"And sometimes I get embarrassed," Nels added.

"Embarrassed? Embarrassed about what?"

"Well, like, when kids ask me what I'm going to get for Christmas, I can't tell them that I'm not getting anything at all. So, I just lie about it, and tell them that I don't know what I'll be getting."

"Nels, I have never deprived you of anything. Since when have we needed Christmas for you to get gifts? Any time you've ever really wanted something, as long as it was within reason, I've gotten it for you. And if you stop to think about it, that has to be better than Christmas, doesn't it? All the other kids have to wait a whole year for Christmas to roll around before they get what they want."

"Yes, that's nice, but Christmas isn't just the gifts. It's all the other things."

"What other things?"

"All the decorations."

"Well, you sure aren't being denied decorations," Galen replied with a snort that might have been a laugh. "All you have to do is look around you. There isn't a building, pole, or protrusion up here that doesn't have some sort of Christmas decoration."

"But it isn't just that, either," Nels went on. "It's everything about

Christmas. It's the way people treat each other. Everyone is nice to everyone else. And they smile a lot."

"Well, smiles are good," Galen agreed.

"And it's the anticipation."

"Anticipation?" Galen laughed. "That's a pretty big word for you, isn't it?"

"Yes. Miss Springer taught it to us. It means that you are waiting eagerly for something."

"I see."

"On the chalkboard in front of our room there's a big number that is the number of days left before Christmas. Every day Miss Springer changes it, so that it goes down one more number. And when she does, everyone gets just that much more excited. Miss Springer says that is anticipation." Nels was quiet for a moment. "But I don't feel the same excitement the other kids do."

"Well, they are getting excited because that means they'll be getting their gifts. But I've already told you that you can have anything . . . within reason, without having to wait."

"That's just it, Dad. Since I don't have to wait for anything, I don't have anything to get excited about. And I would kind of like to get excited like the other kids."

"I didn't know you felt that way about Christmas. You've never told me."

"I guess I never really knew what I was missing until now. But when I see the way everyone else is acting about all this, it makes me feel like I'm missing out on something."

"I see." Galen took a swallow of his coffee. "Where is this play being performed? At the church?"

"No, it will be in the auditorium at school. Miss Springer says there's no other place else in town large enough to hold everyone. So we'll do it in the school gym."

"I just can't believe that the entire village is going to come to the school auditorium to watch a play put on by a bunch of fourth graders."

"Yes, they are," Nels said. "But it isn't just the play, Dad. It's everything. The village celebration is being held in the school auditorium."

"What village celebration?"

"I can't believe you haven't heard of this, Dad," Nels said fiercely. "I mean, with everybody getting ready and everything. They've been talking about it at school ever since we got here. See, every year there's a big Christmas party in the school gym, and the whole village shows up. They all eat Christmas dinner together, then they play games."

"What kind of games?"

Nels laughed. "That's the really funny part, Dad. They have an ear pull, where they pull on each other's ear until someone gives up. And they do a little finger pull. And a one-legged kick. Toby Talitalira is really good at the one-legged kick, but every time I try it, I fall right on my butt. And there'll be a big tug-of-war. But Miss Springer says the most important thing will be our Nativity play. That's what it's called, Dad. A Nativity play, because it's about the birth of Jesus."

"In the school auditorium," Galen said again.

"Yes, in the school auditorium."

"Nels, I want you to tell Miss Springer that you won't be in her play. And we won't be attending any of the ceremonies."

"What?" Nels asked, clearly shocked by his father's words.

"You know how I feel about Christmas. When you're an adult, you can celebrate Christmas any way you wish. But for now, I would like for you to honor my wishes. I don't want either one of us to have anything to do with whatever celebration the school, or the village, has planned."

"Dad! You can't do that!" Nels said, his voice pleading his case. "We've been practicing. Everyone is depending on me! Miss Springer is depending on me!"

"I'm sure she can get someone else."

"No, she can't. Not now. Dad, please! It's too late for her to get someone else."

"Why is it too late? You said yourself that you didn't have any lines to memorize. If all you're doing is reading from the Bible, anyone can do that."

"No, they can't," Nels said. Though he wasn't sobbing out loud, tears were sliding down his cheeks. "Miss Springer said I was doing it because I was the best."

"I'm sure you are the best. And I'm sure she will recognize that talent and find another play for you to be in. But I don't want you to be in this one."

"It's not just a play, it's an assignment. If I'm not in the play, I'll get an F."

"No, you won't. Tikigaq is a public school. And public schools are not supposed to have anything that deals with religion. That's a federal law. So that means that she can't make you be in this play. Furthermore, if you refuse, she can't do anything to you. And she certainly cannot give you an F."

"What will I tell the kids in my class?" Nels pleaded.

"Why do you have to tell them anything? Just tell them that . . . tell them that you and I have something else planned for Christmas."

"They won't believe me."

"Okay, maybe they won't believe you when you tell them. But they'll certainly believe you when you don't show up. And trust me, Nels. You aren't going to show up," Galen added pointedly.

"All right, boys and girls, put away your seatwork now and let's get ready for the full dress rehearsal. Stagehands, you are excused to go to the gym, to get the set ready. Actors, you can get into your costumes.

The rest of you, if you have nothing to do with the play, go get into the bleachers. You are our test audience."

There was a bustle of activity as everyone hurried to respond to Ellie's instructions. Several stopped by to ask questions about last-minute details and she dealt with them one by one. Then, as the last person left the room and Ellie was clearing off her desk, she saw that Nels was still sitting at his desk.

"Nels, you'd better hurry to get into your own costume," she said. "You're up first, remember."

"I can't be in the play," Nels said quietly.

Ellie looked up from her desk. "I beg your pardon? What did you just say?"

"I can't be in the play," Nels repeated. "Dad said I couldn't."

"What do you mean? Of course you can. I picked you for a very important role."

"Miss Springer, is this play religious?"

"Well, yes, of course it is," Ellie said. "It's a play about the birth of Christ, which also makes it a play about the birth of Christianity. So, yes, in answer to your question, the play is religious."

"Then Dad said you can't make me be in it."

Ellie began drumming her fingers on the desk. So that was what this was about. Galen had made a few disparaging comments about Christmas, but she just assumed he was against the crass commercialism of the holiday. She had no idea he was against the entire thing.

Ellie sighed. "Your father is right," she finally said. "I can't make you be in the play."

"Oh," Nels said, clearly disappointed. "I was sort of hoping that you could."

"Perhaps if I talk to your father?" Ellie suggested.

"You can try, but it won't do any good," Nels insisted.

Ellie smiled. "You and your father are coming to my house for dinner tonight. I'll talk to him then."

"Uhmm, that was good pumpkin pie," Galen said. "And I'll be honest with you—I generally don't like pumpkin pie. I was only going to eat it so as not to be rude, but that was delicious."

Ellie smiled. "Well, I wish I could take credit for it, or say that it was an old recipe of my mother's or something. But the truth is, I learned how to make it from Molly Kowanna. This is her recipe."

"It is? I wonder why she has never served it to us."

"Well, you'll get your fill of it at the big village Christmas Festival," Ellie said. "Every year, she makes about twenty pies. It's one of the best things there."

"The Christmas Festival," Galen said.

"Yes. Oh, wait until you see it," Ellie said enthusiastically. "It is one of the most wonderful things ever. It's a true cultural event."

Galen looked over at Nels, who was playing with Maggie. Despite Galen's stare, Nels wouldn't look up to meet his father's gaze. Instead, he continued to rub the dog behind her ears.

Galen took a deep breath, then let it out slowly. "Nels, you didn't tell Miss Springer?"

"I told her, Dad," Nels said, mumbling the words so quietly that Galen had to strain to hear them.

"Do you mean, did he tell me that you don't want him to be in the play?" Ellie asked. "Yes, he told me that, but I assumed you were talking about the play, not the entire festival. And I was hoping that I could talk you into changing your mind about not letting him be in the play. You would be very proud of him, Galen. He reads beautifully."

Galen sighed. "I'm glad you are pleased with his reading. But I'm not changing my mind. He won't be in the play, and we won't be attending the Christmas celebration."

Ellie reached out to put her hand on Galen's. "Oh, Galen," she said. "You can't mean that. I mean, all right, you don't want him to be in the play . . . I can understand that. Well, no, to be honest, I can't even understand that, but he is your son, after all, and I respect your wishes. But please don't get the play confused with the village festival. The festival is much more than a Christmas celebration. I told you, it's a genuine cultural event. I can't believe you would let him come up here and not allow him this experience."

"Believe it, Miss Springer," Galen said. "Neither my son nor I will take part in any Christmas activities. Certainly not in a public school."

Ellie jerked her hand back as if it had been burned. His use of Miss Springer, rather than Ellie, went straight to her heart.

"I should have realized the other night, when we were talking about the northern lights and you took issue with the idea that God might take a personal interest in anyone, that you are an atheist. If so, then just overlook the religious aspects of the celebration and see it as an educational experience."

"My religious belief has nothing to do with it," Galen said.

"Then, what does?"

"He knows," Galen said, nodding toward Nels, who was still playing with the dog. "Nels, tell your teacher why we don't celebrate Christmas."

"It's because of Mom," Nels said.

"Because of your mother? I . . . . I thought she was dead."

"She is dead, and that's the point," Galen said.

Ellie looked at Galen with an expression of total confusion on her face. She shook her head. "I'm afraid I still don't understand. What, exactly, is the point?"

"How do you think it is going to make Nels feel, if he sees all the other children happy, laughing, running to their mother to show her something, when he has no mother? I'm sure you've read articles about it, how depression can be greatly intensified during these periods of public gaiety."

"Well, yes, I have."

"I don't want that to happen to Nels."

"I can understand your sentiment, Galen, but not your reasoning," Ellie said. "It's a tragedy that Nels lost his mother. But she will be gone for the rest of his life. I think you are doing him a disservice by trying to protect him from that. Who knows—something like this might just be very good for him."

"I think I know what is best for my own son," Galen said. "We will not be attending the Christmas celebration, and that is final."

"I'm sorry to hear that," Ellie said.

Galen stood. "Nels, come. I think it's time we went home."

It wasn't until then that Ellie noticed Nels was crying. He rubbed his eyes with his fist, wiping away the tears.

"Good night, Miss Springer," Nels said.

"Good night, Nels," Ellie replied.

Galen and Ellie did not exchange good nights.

~ Twelve ~

Ellie watched through the window as Galen and Nels climbed onto the snowmobile for the drive back home. Maggie had jumped up on the chair beside her, and was also looking through the window. Absently, Ellie began rubbing the dog behind the ears.

"Who was that, Maggie?" she said. "It certainly wasn't the Galen Scobey I thought I knew."

Then she remembered some of the conversation they'd had upon leaving the Whaler's Café.

"Are you saying God never takes a personal interest in anyone, or anything?"

"Yeah, that's pretty much what I'm saying." (There had been a hint of bitterness in his voice.)

"You have been hurt, haven't you?"

"Let's don't talk about it anymore."

"Oh, Maggie. He *has* been hurt. He's been hurt badly."

*   *   *

When they got back to their room, Nels went right to bed.

"Aren't you going to watch television?" Galen asked.

"I don't feel like it."

"Nels, try to understand."

"Good night, Dad," Nels said. He rolled over in his bed, turning his back to his father.

Galen looked at him for a moment, then sighed. If Nels didn't want to talk about it, he wasn't going to force him.

Galen opened one of the folders and began examining the shot reports. But though his eyes were looking at the graphs and charts, the information wasn't being processed by his brain. Instead, he was remembering.

"I forgot your Christmas present," Julia said. "It's still in the car."

"It's raining and cold. There's no need for you to have to go out there. If you want, I'll get it for you," Galen offered.

"Ha! You wish. You just want to see what I got you, that's all. You're not fooling me, Galen Scobey. Not for one minute."

"What are you talking about? I'm just being nice, that's all. I've made a pot of coffee and it's decaf. Why don't you just sit there and have a cup? I'll go get the present and be right back in. And I won't peek, I promise."

Galen started toward the front door, but Julia stepped in front of him and held her hand up like a traffic cop. "That's not going to happen. You stay here and drink the coffee. I'll get the gift from the car," she said, pointedly, as she began putting on her raincoat.

"Come on, Julia, you aren't being fair," Galen complained. "After all, you know what I got you for Christmas."

"Yes, but that's because you told me. And did I ask you to tell me? No, I did not. You just couldn't keep it secret." She laughed. "I swear, when it comes to Christmas, I've got two kids, Nels and you. And you

are worse than Nels because he's too young to know what it's all about."

"All right, go get my present. I was just trying to be nice to you. There's a football game I want to watch anyway. The only thing, when you start freezing your tail off, don't forget that I made the offer."

"Nice try," Julia said as she opened her umbrella, then went outside.

Galen looked through the window until Julia reached the car. He thought he might be able to see something when she took it out of the car; but instead of taking something out, she got in. Realizing then that he wasn't going to be able to see anything, he walked back over to the couch, picked up the remote, and turned the game on.

The game he had chosen was one of the pre–New Year's Day bowl games. But, even though it was a lesser bowl, as the two teams, Alabama and Nebraska, were nearly evenly matched, it proved to be very exciting. Galen got into the game quickly, and it wasn't until the end of the first quarter that he realized Julia hadn't come back inside. He chuckled.

"You didn't have to go next door to wrap the present," he said under his breath. "Do you think I'm so bad that I would peek?"

Even as he asked the question, he knew that, if he was honest with himself, the answer would be yes.

Julia teased him about how much a kid he was over Christmas. And maybe that was so. But he had been raised by a single mother who, though money was always tight, had always managed to make Christmas something special.

Once, when he was old enough to realize what an effort it had to be for her, he suggested that he would understand if she didn't buy him a gift.

"Don't worry about it," his mother told him, kissing him on the forehead. "Don't you understand? No matter how tight money is, we'll always be able to celebrate Christmas, because there's something magic about this time of year."

Julia was probably next door, right now, telling Gina how she needed *to hide from Galen to wrap his present. He picked up the phone and dialed. Ed Davis, his next-door neighbor, answered.*

"Hi, Ed, this is Galen. Let me talk to Julia, would you?"

"Julia? Well, I don't think she's here, Galen, but I'll check," Ed said.

Galen heard Ed question Gina, then he came back to the phone. "No, Julia isn't here. Gina says she hasn't seen her since early this afternoon."

Galen was surprised and a little concerned. If Julia wasn't over there, where was she?

"Okay, Ed, thanks."

He hung up the phone, then walked back over to the kitchen door to look out toward the driveway. Julia's car was still there. He couldn't tell if she was still inside the car or not, though, because the rain prevented him from seeing through the car windows.

When he opened the door, he heard the tympani of falling rain, from the rhythmic percussion of the large booming drops to the delicate trill of the water that ran off the roof and cascaded across the eaves. Though there was a small overhang that protected him, some of the rain was blowing into his face, and while not quite freezing, it was very cold.

"Julia? Julia, are you still out here?"

Surely not. It was much too uncomfortable for her to be outside this long, even in the car. But if she wasn't in the car, where was she? As his concerned curiosity grew to more concern than curiosity, he walked out into the rain.

"Julia?" he called again.

He opened the car door.

That was when he saw her. A half-wrapped package was in her lap, her head was back on the seat, and her eyes were open but unseeing.

With an effort, Galen jerked his thoughts back to the present. But the memory had been so powerful that, for a brief moment, a part of him refused to abandon it. Then, gradually, he felt himself returning to reality. He wasn't in Dallas, he was in Point Hope, Alaska, seven years after the event.

The heater fan made a clicking sound as it came on, and a column of warm air started pushing back the chill of the room.

On the desk, the large, glowing red numbers of a digital clock marked the time as 11:14. In the bed across the room from him, Nels's measured breathing indicated he was sleeping soundly.

Galen pinched the bridge of his nose, trying to push away the memories. And yet, for a long, lingering moment, the terrible image of his wife, collapsed in the front seat of her car, stayed with him.

Julia had died from an aneurism. The doctor told Galen that it had been mercifully quick, and that she had probably felt no more pain than she would with the onset of an ordinary headache.

"I should've checked on her," Galen said, berating himself. "I got interested in the ball game and didn't realize she hadn't come back inside. If I had just gone out there sooner, maybe I could've done something to help her."

"No, there is nothing you could have done except watch her die," the doctor said. "And I don't think you would have wanted that."

"No," Galen agreed.

"Then quit beating yourself to death over it. Some things are just God's will."

"God's will? To take Julia from her husband and baby during this season that is supposed to be so holy? What kind of God would do such a thing?"

Dr. Urban clucked, and shook his head. "I'm afraid that's a question of theology, not medicine."

Julia was taken back to her hometown of Sikeston, Missouri, for burial, and as it turned out, her funeral was held on Christmas Eve.

After the service in the church, Galen climbed into the backseat of the funeral limousine for the ride to the cemetery. Nels, who was but a month over two years old, was too young to understand what had happened. He was sitting beside his father.

The cortège wound its way through the center of town, and as they passed an arc of Corinthian columns—all that was left of a church that burned many years earlier—Nels looked up, smiled broadly, and pointed.

"Mama!" he said.

"What?"

"Mama! Light!" Nels smiled broadly as he pointed at the large decorative lighted star that sat on top of the columns.

The star he was pointing to was much larger than the one Julia had bought for the tree and shown to Nels. But there was such a marked similarity between this star and Julia's that Nels had made the connection between the two.

Nels got a puzzled expression on his face as if wondering again why his mother wasn't with him.

"Where Mama?" he asked. Standing in the seat, he looked through the back window at the cars following. "Mama, where?"

Galen took Nels, wrapped his arms around him, and pulled him close, so that the boy's head was on his shoulder. That way, Nels couldn't see him crying.

Galen stared, with tear-filled eyes, through the dark-shaded window of the car, at the ongoing gaiety of the season: the happy Christmas shoppers hurrying to buy those last-minute gifts, the lights and greenery that decorated the downtown lamps, the holiday displays adorning every store window in town.

Then he closed his eyes so he wouldn't have to see these symbols of cheer, so painfully incongruous with what he was feeling.

The cortège reached the Garden of Memories Cemetery, then stopped. A series of doors slammed as those who had come to the funeral left their cars and came over to stand around the open grave, and the green-and-white-striped awning that had been erected at the graveside.

Galen sat in the front row of chairs, along with Julia's mother and father. He held Nels on his lap as the Episcopal priest began the liturgy of the committal.

The priest stood at the head of the coffin. *"All that the Father giveth me shall come to me; and him that cometh to me I will in no wise cast out."*

The grave was at the very edge of the cemetery. Separated from the cemetery by a narrow hedge was a small brick house. During the service a car pulled into the driveway of that house and, amidst the opening and closing of doors, those arriving in the car and those living in the house greeted each other effusively in the front yard.

"Oh, you're here! You made it!"

"Merry Christmas!"

"Merry Christmas! How was your drive down?"

"Awful. Traffic on Fifty-five never let up, from St. Louis to here."

"He that raised up Jesus from the dead will also give life to our mortal bodies, by His Spirit that dwelleth in us."

"Have you heard from Edna?"

"Yes, she'll be here for dinner."

"In sure and certain hope of the resurrection to eternal life through our Lord Jesus Christ, we commend to Almighty God, our sister, Julie, and we commit her body to the ground, earth to earth, ashes to ashes, dust to dust."

"Oh, my, they're having a funeral. It must be awful to have a funeral on Christmas Eve."

"Pay no attention to it. When you live next to a cemetery, you get used to these things. They don't bother us and we don't bother them. Come on inside."

"The God of Peace, who brought again from the dead our Lord Jesus Christ, the great Shepherd of the sheep, through the blood of the everlasting covenant: Make you perfect in every good work to do His will, working in you that which is well pleasing in His sight; through Jesus Christ, to whom be glory for ever and ever. Amen."

When the service ended, the priest stepped up to take Galen's hand in his.

"I am so sorry for your loss," he said. "I didn't know Julie . . . "

"Julia," Galen corrected.

"Julia," the priest said. "As I say, I didn't know her, she left Sikeston before I became rector of St. Paul's. But those who did know her have nothing but the highest words of praise for her. And I'm sure that you will take comfort in knowing that she is resting now, in the arms of God."

"There is no God," Galen said bitterly.

Once again pushing away the memories, Galen got up and walked over to look through the window. Across the street from the bed and breakfast, a string of glowing colored lights outlined the roof of the Native Store. The lights reflected back from the snow in little gleaming patches of red, green, blue, and yellow.

"What a foolish and delusional waste of electricity," he said under his breath. "How can the Christ Child be the Son of God, when there is no God?"

He turned away from the window and walked over to Nels's bed. Sitting on the edge of the bed, he leaned over to embrace his son. Nels didn't awaken.

"Nels, I know you can't understand, and won't understand what I'm going to do. But I think the best thing now is to just stop this whole business. I can only hope that, someday, you will be able to for-give me."

It had been long enough since Julia died that Galen didn't have these bad moments very often. But when he did have them, they were hard to shake. And nothing could bring them out as vividly as Christmas.

~ *Thirteen* ~

When Clay Berber opened the door to his room at the Whalers' Inn, the expression on his face registered his surprise at seeing Galen Scobey.

"Mr. Scobey," he said. His eyes narrowed suspiciously. "What are you doing here?"

"May I come in, Mr. Berber? There is something I would like to talk to you about."

"Yeah? Well, I'll save you the trouble. Your position up here is too strong. There's nothing left for me, so I'm leaving today."

"There may be something else for you to do up here. That is, if you are interested," Galen said.

"What?"

"Aren't you getting a little cold, standing here with the door open?" Galen made a gesture indicating that he would like to come in.

"Oh, yeah," Berber said. He stepped away from the door. "All right, come on in."

"Thanks."

Berber's open suitcase was on the bed, and he was throwing clothes into it, packing for his trip back home.

"What is it, Scobey? What's on your mind?" Berber asked, as he resumed his packing.

"Mr. Berber, I would like to hire your legal services."

"Is that it? Is that what you wanted to talk to me about?"

"Yes."

Berber shook his head. "Well, you could've saved yourself the time and bother of coming over. I cannot, and I will not work for you, my friend."

"Why not?"

"Because whether you believe me or not, I am sincere in the causes that I fight for. And it would be a betrayal of everything I have ever done if I suddenly reversed myself and represented big oil. Besides, I told you, you don't need a lawyer. Your position up here is unassailable. I know when I'm licked. I will not be able to get to you through the courts."

"Mr. Berber, the reason I want to hire you has nothing to do with the company I work for, or the project I'm working on. In fact, it has nothing at all to do with oil."

"Then why *do* you want to hire me?"

"How do you feel about the separation of church and state?" Galen asked.

"Is that a trick question?"

"No, I'm very serious. How do you feel about the separation of church and state?"

"I am a strong advocate of the separation of church and state," Berber said. "You may have read about my case in Mississippi, where I successfully sued to have the Ten Commandments removed from a county courthouse." He chuckled. "It was a stone engraving that had been up there since 1847, and the lawyer for the other side tried to argue that it was part of the county's historical heritage. But I beat him."

"Good."

Berber stroked his chin as he studied Galen. He had to admit that the man had piqued his curiosity.

"You want to tell me what this is all about, Scobey?"

"Yeah. I don't know whether you know it or not, but every year the village of Point Hope holds a Christmas Festival that involves just about everyone in town. I don't want anything to do with it, and I don't want my son to have anything to do with it, either."

Berber went back to packing. "Nothing wrong with that," he said. "People have a right to celebrate Christmas if they want to. If you don't want to go, don't go. It's as simple as that."

"No, it isn't as simple as that."

"Why not?"

"Because here, the Christmas Festival is held in the school gym."

Once again Berber interrupted his packing to look up at Galen. "The public school gym?"

"Tikigaq is the only school here," Galen said. "Yes, it is a public school. Go down and see for yourself. They have it all decorated and everything."

"And you're telling me that they're actually holding a Christmas celebration in a public school?" Berber said. He shook his head. "No, that's a violation of the Constitution. They can't do that."

"So it would seem," Galen agreed. "But whether they can or not, they've done it. And that puts me in a very difficult situation. Because if they have it and I don't allow my son to participate, he might very well be ostracized."

"Oh, yes, I'm sure he would be ostracized," Berber said. "That's exactly why this has come up before. People who don't consider themselves Christians often feel left out during Christmas. And something like this just makes it worse. It's only by eliminating all vestiges of Christmas from any public arena that we can guarantee the rights of all."

"Will you take the job?"

His suitcase packed, Berber closed it, then snapped it shut. He studied Galen for a long moment.

"I don't get it," he said. "I came here to try and stop you. Now you want to hire me."

"You weren't here to stop me, personally," Galen pointed out. "You were here to defend a principle you believe in. Well, I believe in a clean environment just as much as you do. But I think that should be balanced with the public's need for a safe, economic source of energy. So, on that point we differ.

"On the other hand, I have never taken issue with the dedication you have to the service of conscience and right. And on the issue of the separation of church and state, we are in total agreement." Galen smiled. "I figure that if a person takes the time to do a little research, they will always find that there are more things that unite them than there are that divide them."

Berber smiled. "That's a good line," he said. "I'll have to remember that."

"Will you do it?"

"Are you prepared to pay the price?"

"Yes. I don't know what you charge but—"

Berber held up his hand, interrupting Galen in midsentence.

"That's not the price I'm talking about," he said. "Someone who in an act of conscience fights to have religion eliminated from the public arena will always pay a very heavy price. And in this case, since, as you say, the entire village is a willing participant, your price will be particularly high."

"I'm sure there will be some who won't approve of me for doing this."

"You will be vilified, demonized, and hated. And I can't promise that you won't be in danger. Are you prepared for all of that?"

"I want this Christmas celebration stopped, whatever it takes," Galen said resolutely.

Berber stared at Galen for a long moment, then he stuck out his hand.

"You've just hired yourself a lawyer," he said.

Two days after the meeting between Galen and Berber, Ellie was at her desk when Sunshine Komack brought her a note from the principal, Sam Keating.

"Thank you, Miss Komack," Ellie said, smiling at the young Eskimo teachers' assistant.

"You won't thank me when you read it," Sunshine said glumly.

"Oh? Why do you say that?"

"You will see."

Ellie opened the note and read:

NOTICE TO ALL TEACHERS:

Due to a filing made by Mr. Galen Scobey, a federal judge of the District Court has issued a writ *pro tempore*. The effect of this writ will prevent Tikigaq School from participating in, promoting, or even recognizing Christmas. Accordingly, all Christmas decorations must be removed from the classrooms, and Christmas activities, such as the Nativity play and choral concert, are hereby canceled. In addition, we will not be allowed to make our facility available for the village celebration.

Ellie folded the note over, slid it under the blotter, then began drumming her fingers on the desk. For a long moment, she looked out at her students. They were all gathered at the back of the room, working on the set for the Nativity play. They were very proud of their work so far, and rightfully so.

From scrap lumber, they had constructed a realistic-looking stable, complete with a straw-filled manger. Behind the stable, in bas-relief made of papier-mâché, were the domes and roofs of old Bethlehem. And beyond the papier-mâché village could be seen painted hills, fields, flocks of sheep, and a midnight sky, filled with stars. The children had also painted in the northern lights, which Ellie allowed because she felt that it gave them a more personal connection.

Originally, the Star of Bethlehem was to have been painted in as well, but Nels came up with the idea that they use a real light instead. He had fashioned the star by putting a bright light inside a frosted-glass bowl. The arms of the star were made from clear plastic, glued to the bowl in such a way as to extend the light.

"I got the idea from the big star over Reunion Tower in Dallas," Nels told Ellie as he undertook the project.

"Oh, yes, I know that light. It's very pretty at night," Ellie said.

"That's where my mom is," Nels said, matter-of-factly.

"I beg your pardon?"

"My mom," Nels said again. He laughed. "Well, she's not actually in the light. But every time I see it, I think of her."

"Oh, what a wonderful thing to think and feel," Ellie said. "Yes, by all means, you can make the star."

Ellie had to admit that Nels had done a very good job with his star.

"Boys and girls," Ellie called.

So involved were they with their activities that they didn't hear her the first time she called.

"Boys and girls!" she repeated, a little louder this time.

Now they interrupted their work to look toward her.

"Would you—uh—take your seats, please?"

"But, Miss Springer, we aren't finished," one of the boys said.

"I know. Please, just take your seats," she said again.

The children all returned to their seats.

"I've just received a note from Mr. Keating," Ellie said. "We have been told that we must stop all Christmas activity."

"You mean we are supposed to stop before we are finished?" Rex Hale said.

"Yes."

"Why?" Daisy Koonook asked.

Ellie took a deep breath, then let out a long sigh. "Because we have been ordered to stop, that's why." It wasn't a very good answer, Ellie knew. But at this point she didn't want to tell her class that Nels's father was responsible for all this. They were going to find out soon enough, and when they did, it would be hard on Nels. She hoped to spare him the grief for as long as she could.

"Miss Springer, does this mean we aren't going to do the play?" Rex asked. Rex was portraying Joseph, and he was particularly proud of his important role.

"Yes, I'm afraid that is what it means. No play, no music, and no Christmas decorations," Ellie said.

"But we've already got Christmas decorations up," Daisy said.

"Yes, but we'll just have to take everything down, that's all. The set for the play, and all the decorations."

"But why?"

"We have been ordered to do so."

"But, if Mr. Keating takes down all the decorations, how will the village have its festival?" one of the children asked.

"Yes," Daisy said. "You've got to have Christmas decorations for the festival."

"You don't understand," Ellie said sadly. "There will be no Christmas Festival this year."

When Galen came back from the tundra late that same afternoon, he stopped at the Native Store to refuel his snowmobile. Luke Koonook, Mark Hale, Isaac Ahlook, and Percy Tokomik were there, talking to John Kingik, the manager of the store.

"Hi, guys, how's it going?" Galen asked as he took out his billfold. "Here you go, John. I had eighteen dollars and twenty-three cents worth of gas," he said, handing over a twenty-dollar bill to Kingik.

"Ask him, John," Mark Hale said.

"Yeah, ask him. I want to see what he says," Tokomik added.

It wasn't until then that Galen was aware the others were glaring at him.

"Ask me what? What's going on?"

"Is it true?" Kingik asked as he made change.

"Is what true?"

"Are you responsible for shutting down the Christmas Festival?" Kingik asked.

Galen was surprised by the question. It had only been a couple of days since he approached Berber with the request that he take the matter to court. He was amazed at how quick the response was. Give the devil his due, Galen thought, once Clay Berber got his teeth into a project, he didn't waste any time.

"Well, are you going to answer the question or not?" Hale asked.

"I didn't have anything to do with shutting the festival down," Galen said.

Mark Hale smiled, and looked at the others. "See, I told you Mr. Scobey wouldn't have anything to do with that. Why, my dad wouldn't work for him if he was responsible for that."

Galen took a deep breath.

"I didn't try to stop the festival," he continued. "All I did was protest the fact that it was going to be held in a public school gym. That is a violation of the separation of church and state, so I filed a petition with the federal court to have it moved."

The smile left Hale's face.

"Then you *are* responsible," he said.

"I'm responsible only for changing the location. I made no suggestion that the event be canceled," Galen protested.

"That's the same thing," Ahlook said.

"No, it isn't the same thing," Galen insisted. "I said nothing about canceling the festival."

"Don't you understand?" Koonook asked. "The school gym is the only place large enough to hold the festival. If we're forced to move it out of the gym, then we will have to cancel it."

"Luke, you are the mayor of Point Hope. You of all people should know that you can't use a public school for a religious event," Galen said. "That's under the protection guaranteed us by the U.S. Constitution, requiring a separation between church and state. You have an obligation to protect the right of every one of your citizens."

"None of my citizens has ever complained before," Koonook said.

"Well, maybe nobody else has had reason to complain," Galen said. "I do."

"You have no business complaining, anyway," Tokomik growled. "You aren't one of the citizens of Point Hope."

"I don't have to be a citizen of Point Hope to file this complaint,

Mr. Tokomik. All I have to be is a citizen of the United States, and that I am."

"So what you are telling us is that anyone in the country, just because they are an American citizen, can come up here and start changing our laws around?" Hale asked.

"Yes, because this isn't one of your laws. This is a federal law . . . a law designed to protect all the citizens of the United States," Galen said pointedly.

Suddenly John Kingik came out from behind the counter. He started chanting something in Eskimo, all the while dancing around Galen, pointing at him with one hand and waving the other.

"What is this? What's going on?" Galen asked.

"John is an *afatkug*," Koonook said.

"A what?"

"An *afatkug*," Koonook said again. "Some people call them shamans."

With a final loud shout and a dramatic wave of his hands, Kingik threw something on the floor in front of Galen. It bounced off the floor, hit Galen's leg, then fell back.

For a long moment, everyone was very quiet. Galen looked at all of them, trying to figure out what was going on. Finally he reached down to pick up the thing Kingik had thrown. Looking at it, he saw that it was some sort of animal, though he couldn't identify what kind it was.

He started to hand it back to Kingik, but Kingik turned his back.

"What is it?" Galen asked. "What is all this about?"

"He has given it to you," Mark Hale said.

"Why? I doubt that I have made any friends by what I did."

He examined the little effigy more carefully. It had an open mouth, full of teeth.

"What kind of animal is this, anyway?"

"It's a *tikituk*," Tokomik said.

"A *tikituk*?" Galen shook his head. "I've never heard of a *tikituk*."

"It's a spirit animal," Hale said. "The *afatkug* has just put a spell on you."

For the third time in as many weeks, nearly everyone in the village turned out for a meeting at the school gym. Most had heard only rumors about the subject of the meeting, and they didn't like the rumors they were hearing.

Mayor Luke Koonook stepped up to the podium and raised his hands, calling for quiet. Over a few dangling conversations, smothered coughs, and scraping chairs, the auditorium gradually became quiet. It was so silent that they could hear the fans circulating the heated air.

"I know there are a lot of rumors going around town about what happened to the Christmas celebration," Koonook began. "So I may as well start this meeting off by telling you that the rumors are true. We won't be able to hold the Christmas Festival in the gym this year."

"What?"

"Why not?"

"Oh no!"

"So, what do we do now?"

Koonook waited until the cries of amazement and anger quieted before he continued.

"We knew that we were on thin ice by holding the festival in the gym. All over the lower forty-eight, there have been court actions saying that schools can't celebrate Christmas.

"But we thought that since nobody up here had ever complained, and that we were all in this together, we would be safe."

"Who did complain, Luke?"

"Well, I don't want to get into that now," Koonook replied. "The point is, someone did complain, and now we have a temporary injunction saying that we cannot use the school for our celebration."

One of the men on the stage was Father Greg Tobin, rector of St. Thomas's Episcopal Church.

"What about holding it in the church parish hall, Father Greg?" Gus Kowanna asked.

"Of course, I will gladly make the parish hall available," Father Tobin replied. "But I'm sure you know it holds less than two hundred people, and then it's so crowded you can barely move. We normally have about seven hundred attend the fest."

"It was Scobey, wasn't it?" someone from the crowd shouted. "Scobey is the one who complained."

"I told you, I'd rather not say," Koonook responded.

"You don't have to say," another voice said. "I know it was Scobey. And here, after we voted a second time to let him look for oil. How do you like that? We took him in and he stabbed us in the back!"

"Where is he now?" someone asked.

"I don't know," Koonook said.

"Well, he's not here, that's for sure. Shows what a coward he is. He won't even face up to us and tell us why he's doing this."

"It doesn't matter who did it or why it was done," Koonook replied. "All that matters is it was done. Which means that we will not have a Christmas Festival this year. And it also means no Christmas decorations."

"What about the new star?" Isaac Ahlook asked.

"What new star?" Koonook replied.

"Come on, Luke, you know about it," Ahlook said. "The city council voted on it. It cost us over a thousand dollars. I'd hate not to be able to use it."

"It's over here," Henry Killigivuk said, pointing to a huge crystal ball on the stage.

"Holy Cow! That thing is as big as the light they drop at Times Square every year," Koonook said.

Ahlook laughed. "That's why we can only put it up at Christmas. If we put it up in the summertime, the ships would think it was a lighthouse."

"What about it, Mayor? Can we put it up?" Tokomik asked.

"Under the circumstances, I'm afraid not," Koonook said soberly. "And all the other decorations that are at the school, or on public property, will have to come down."

"What about the school play?" someone asked. "We'll still be able to do that, won't we?"

Koonook shook his head. "No. As far as Point Hope is concerned, you just have to get used to the fact that there will be no Christmas this year. In fact, there may never be another Christmas for us."

～ Fourteen ～

Luke Koonook, Mark Hale, Sam Keating, and Ellie Springer were in the pastor's study at St. Thomas's. Father Tobin offered them their choice of coffee or tea; then, when all were attended to, he sat down as well.

"What's up, Father Greg?" Mark asked. "On the telephone, you said you had an idea."

"I do," Tobin replied. He held up a little sheet of paper. "Luke, is this the fax you received from Judge Fugate of the District Court?"

Mayor Koonook took the paper and examined it for a moment. "Yes, that's it," he said, handing it back.

"So far as you know, is this the *only* order that has been issued, barring us from using the school?" Father Tobin asked.

"Well, yes, but how many do you need?" Koonook replied. "It says we can't do it."

"Well, no, if you examine it closely, it doesn't exactly say that. This is a writ *pro tempore,* not a court order."

"A writ *pro tempore*? What does that mean?"

Tobin smiled. "That means that Judge Fugate didn't want to make the final decision. So he got around it by issuing a temporary injunction until further study could determine the final outcome."

"Wait a minute," Ellie said. "Are you saying that this ruling could be overturned?"

"That is exactly what I'm saying. That is, if we could present our case to the appeals court."

"Where is this appeals court you're talking about?" Mark Hale asked. "Anchorage?"

"No, it's in San Francisco," Sam Keating said.

"San Francisco? Oh yeah, that's a real hotbed of conservatism," Mark said. "I'm sure we'll find a lawyer there to argue our case!"

"I could call the Episcopal Bay Area Diocese," Tobin suggested. "They might suggest a lawyer who could make the appeal for us."

"I know a lawyer in San Francisco," Ellie said.

All eyes turned to her.

"How well do you know him?" Mark asked.

"We went together all through college."

Keating chuckled. "The next question is, how acrimonious was your breakup?"

Everyone laughed, including Ellie.

"No, it wasn't like that. We didn't break up exactly, we just sort of went our own way," she said. "We are still very good friends."

"Do you think he could handle something like this?" Tobin asked. "Or, I suppose I should say, do you think he would handle something like this? Because I'm afraid Mark is right. Most of the lawyers in San Francisco will probably agree with Judge Fugate's decision."

Ellie nodded. "I know he can do it, because he's one of the smartest men I've ever known. And I'm sure he will do it if I ask him. I'll call him."

Father Tobin shook his head. "It's going to take more than a call," he said. "It's going to take your being there, to show the immediacy of our need. Are you willing to take our case to him?"

"Yes, I'll go," Ellie said. "I'll be glad to go." She looked at Keating. "That is, if my boss will give me a few days off."

"I'll do better than that," Keating said. "I'll charge your whole trip off as a school field trip, and pay for it out of school funds."

Bob Bivens stood at the window and stared out over the airfield. The sky was heavily overcast.

"I don't know," he said. "It's looking awfully bad out there."

"Mr. Bivens, I have to be in Kotzebue in time to catch tomorrow's flight out," Ellie said. "It is very important that I get to San Francisco. Please, you've got to take me."

Bivens pointed through the window. "It's bad enough that we won't have anything more than a couple of hours of not much more than twilight. I've checked with Kotzebue weather. There's a fifty percent chance of snow."

"That means there is also a fifty percent chance that there won't be snow," Ellie said.

"Snow could produce a whiteout. You know what a whiteout is, don't you?"

"Yes, I've seen them."

"You want to risk that?"

"I have to catch the plane out of Kotzebue tomorrow."

"You know what pilots call it when you take a chance on weather even though you know better? They call it 'gethomeitis.' That's when your desire to get somewhere overcomes good sense. And that's the kind of thing that can cause you to buy the farm."

"But you don't understand. I *have* to get there," Ellie said again.

"And in case you don't quite grasp the significance of what I just said, young lady, most of the time when the pilot buys the farm, the passengers flying with him get killed also," Bivens said pointedly.

Ellie walked over to the window and stared out at the gray, drooping sky.

Bivens sighed. "What is so all fired important about you getting to San Francisco, anyway?"

Ellie turned away from the window. "Christmas," she said.

"Christmas?" Bivens replied in an outburst. "You're asking me to risk my neck just so you can get home for Christmas? What's the hurry? It's almost a week until Christmas. The weather is bound to clear before then."

"No, I'm not talking about getting home for Christmas," Ellie said. "I'm talking about saving Christmas for Point Hope."

Bivens looked puzzled for a moment, then he shook his head. "Now I'm totally confused. What in the Sam Hill are you talking about?"

"Mr. Bivens, you have been here for the big Christmas Festival Point Hope has every year, haven't you?"

"Of course I have. Many times. These folks really know how to do it right," Bivens said.

"Well, thanks to Mr. Scobey, they won't be holding the festival this year, or any other year, if he has his say."

"What? Wait a minute, what does he have to say about it, anyway? I thought he was just visiting up here. I mean, isn't he supposed to be looking for oil, or something?"

"Yes. But he has enrolled his son in school here. And he doesn't want his son to be exposed to anything that has to do with Christmas."

"How can he stop it?"

"Well, if you remember, the entire village turns out for the celebration. And the only building in town that is big enough to accommodate everyone is the school gym. Mr. Scobey managed to get a judge to issue an order prohibiting the use of the gym for that purpose. It's a question of separation of church and state."

"Scobey did that?"

"Yes."

"Hmmph. If I'd known that about him, I would never have flown him up here in the first place. So, his kid is the one who caused it all, huh?"

Ellie shook her head. "No, not at all. Nels is in my class. He's a great kid, a wonderful student, and liked by everyone. Or he was until this happened. I'm afraid the other kids aren't treating him very kindly now, since they see him as the reason for not having the Christmas Festival."

"I can't say as I blame them all that much."

"It isn't Nels. It's his father."

"Yeah, but if he didn't have his kid up here with him, none of this would have happened, would it?" Bivens replied. He stared out the window again. "What does your going to San Francisco have to do with getting this changed?"

"I have a friend who is a lawyer there," Ellie answered. "That's where the federal appeals court is."

"And you think your lawyer friend can get this turned around?"

Ellie nodded. "Yes, I think he can. And I know Kevin well enough to know that even if he can't help us, he will find someone who can."

"All right," Bivens said. "I'm a fool for even thinking about it, but if you're willing to put your life on the line for this, then I'll fly you. Come on, let's go."

Ellie smiled broadly. "Oh, thank you, Mr. Bivens. Thank you!" She threw her arms around his neck.

"Hold on," Bivens said, somewhat awkwardly. "Let's see how thankful you'll be if we find ourselves belly-up in the snow somewhere."

Bivens picked up Ellie's suitcase, and they stepped outside into the cold, threatening day and walked toward the plane. As she approached, Ellie got a quick, mental image of the machine twisted and burning somewhere on the snow-covered tundra. Then, closing her eyes to block the image, she opened them again to examine the intact craft with its short, round nose, the two radial engines sticking up in the air, and the fuselage with its row of windows down each side, leading to the tail wing with the twin rudders perched on the small tail wheel. It was an airplane out of time, more like pictures of the airliners Ellie had seen from the 1930s than the twin-engine executive planes of today.

"I'll stow your suitcase; you ride up front with me," Bivens said. "If we go down, I want you to get there just as quickly as I do."

"Gee, thanks," Ellie replied sarcastically.

"I'm just teasing," Bivens said in a softer tone. "But I do want you up there with me because if weather does move in, it might help to have a second pair of eyes."

"Okay. I'll do whatever you ask."

Ellie moved up to the front of the plane, then strapped herself into the right seat. Bivens took the left seat.

"Well, now, let's see if we can get ole *Saigon Sue* into the air," Bivens said as he primed the engine. "Clear!" he called, as he hit the inertia starter toggle.

They reached cruising altitude, then turned south, toward Kotzebue. They were above the clouds now, flying in the dark blue arctic sky.

"We're out of it!" Ellie said happily.

"Not quite," Bivens replied.

"What do you mean? It's clear up here."

Bivens pointed below them. It looked as if the world had been buried under a huge pile of shaving cream.

"That cloud?" Ellie asked.

Bivens nodded. "We're going to have that all the way to Kotzebue," he said. "And when we get there, we will have to let down through it. So get yourself ready."

"If it's no more difficult to go down through it than it was coming up, I'll be all right," Ellie said.

"It's a lot more difficult going down than coming up," Bivens told her soberly.

"Why is that?"

"Coming up, there's nothing to bump into. You pop out of the cloud and you're in clear sky, like we are now. But going down, you could bump into the ground."

The flight to Kotzebue would take about an hour. Ellie settled down for the ride, soothed by the drone of the two engines. Looking out her window, she could see the whirling propeller disk.

Ellie thought about Galen Scobey and tried to understand why he had done what he did. She'd liked him. How could she have been so wrong about him?

No, she didn't think she was wrong about him. Surely there was some reason he was doing this—some reason that she knew nothing about.

Well, whatever his reason, she intended to do everything within her power to see to it that Galen's attempt to prevent Christmas was thwarted. And if her action destroyed any relationship that may have been budding between them, then so be it.

Every five minutes or so Bivens would reach down to turn a dial on the radio, listen for a moment, then turn it back.

"What are you doing?" Ellie asked.

"Kotzebue weather is 135.45," he said. "I'm monitoring it."

"How does it look?"

"Snow hasn't started yet, but they're predicting it any minute."

After the fourth time of changing frequencies, Bivens shook his head and sighed. "I was afraid of that," he said.

"What?"

"We've come down on the wrong side of the fifty percent. It's snowing in Kotzebue."

Seeing the worried expression on Bivens's face, Ellie's nervousness increased. "I'm sorry I talked you into this," she said. "This is all my fault."

"No, it isn't. The final decision was mine, and I made it." He looked over at her and smiled. "But don't worry about it. We've got ILS. We'll be okay."

"ILS?"

"Instrument landing system," he explained. "It'll get us down."

Ellie allowed herself to relax a little. "Good," she said.

They flew on for several more minutes. Bivens checked the weather one more time.

"OTZ, that is, Kotzebue, is reporting whiteout conditions now," he said. He reached down to flip a toggle switch. He flipped it off and on several times, then tapped the instrument panel alongside a dial. "Uh-oh," he said.

"Uh-oh? I don't like to be in an airplane and hear the pilot say that. What's wrong?"

"ILS is out," Bivens said.

"You mean that instrument landing thing you were talking about?"

"Yes."

"Does that mean we can't land?"

Bivens snorted a laugh. "Oh, don't worry about that, honey. We *will* land. In the entire history of aviation, there's never been an airplane left in the sky."

"But how?"

"I don't know—unless—yeah. It might work."

"What? What might work?"

"A ground-controlled approach."

"What's that?"

"It's the way they used to bring planes in back in the old days before ILS. Not many people know how to do it now."

"Do you know how to do it?"

"Oh, yeah," Bivens said confidently. "I know how to do it."

"That's good."

"Problem is, there aren't that many on the ground who know how to do it anymore."

Bivens picked up the microphone.

"Kotzebue Unicom, this is Tango Papa two-one-two. I'm on your VOR, twenty miles north."

"Roger, Tango Papa."

"Say now your weather."

"Ceiling and visibility are zero."

"Uh-huh. How about Kivalina, Noorvik, Kiana, or Selawik? What's the latest from there?"

"Zero, zero," the Unicom operator replied.

"Is Dooley Hawkens around?"

"Dooley? Yes, he's here."

"Get him on, please."

There was about a minute's pause, then another voice came on. "Bob, is this you?"

"Yeah, Dooley, it's me."

"Man, what are you doing up in this stuff? We're socked in here."

"Yeah, I know. Dooley, my ILS is out."

"That's not good."

"No, it's not. So, my friend, I'm going to need you to set up a GCA for me."

"What? That's impossible. We don't have a GCA-calibrated radar system here."

"I know. But you *do* have radar. And you used to do GCAs. I'm hoping that you've handled enough of them that you could figure out some way to sort of wing it."

"Come on, Bob. It's been at least twenty years since I've handled one, maybe longer. And when I did that one I had the system to do it."

"I know. But when you think about it, I don't have much choice here, do I?" Bivens replied.

There was a long beat of silence before Dooley responded. "No, I guess not. Do you have any passengers?"

"Ellie Springer."

"The schoolteacher?"

"Yes."

"Uh-huh. And does she have a next-of-kin we can notify in case something goes wrong?"

"I'm not going to let anything go wrong," Bivens replied resolutely.

"Yeah, well, that's the way to look at it, I suppose."

"I'm committed to OTZ, Dooley. And you're going to have to help me."

"Bob, do you know what you are asking?"

"Yeah, Dooley. I'm asking you to save my life."

There was another pause before Dooley answered. Then he said, "I guess you are at that, aren't you? All right, I'll give it my best shot. Is your fuel critical?"

"I've got about forty-five minutes remaining."

"Better lean out the engines. It's going to take me at least half an hour to try and get something set up, and that doesn't leave you much for maneuvering. Stand by."

"You don't have to worry about that. I'm not going anywhere," Bivens said.

Bivens leaned the fuel mixture back to the point that the engines started to backfire, then he enriched the mixture just enough to keep the engines running.

"Are you a religious woman, Miss Springer?" he asked.

"Yes," Ellie replied.

"Then I take it you know a few prayers?"

"I certainly know how to pray when I'm frightened," Ellie said.

"Yeah, well, I hope you are scared now."

"I am."

"Good. Then pray for all you're worth."

"I've been praying, and I'll keep on praying. Is there anything else I can do?"

"I've leaned the engines out to conserve fuel, but that makes them run hot." Bivens pointed to the cylinder-head temperature gauges. "This is engine one, and this is engine two. If either one of these needles gets into the red arc, let me know."

"Okay," Ellie replied nervously. She was glad she had something to do, something to hold on to and give her a sense of having some control over her own fate.

Bivens began flying in circles while he was waiting for Dooley. Then, after about half an hour, Dooley called him again.

"Tango Papa, set your transponder to C mode, then squawk your parrot so I can get a fix on you."

Bivens reached down to make the adjustment, then moved a toggle switch to emit an identifying signal.

"I read your squawk. Now, come up on 123.6."

"Roger, changing to 123.6," Bivens replied, making the switch.

After changing the radio frequency, he called again. "Kotzebue, this is Tango Papa on 123.6. Are you there?"

"I'm here," Dooley's voice replied. "Okay, Bob, this is what we are going to do. I'm going to use the approach radar to keep you on center-line, and your transponder to establish altitude. Come to heading one-eight-zero."

"One-eight-zero."

"You'll be landing on runway eight. There's a fifteen-foot obstruction, thirty feet from the edge of the runway."

"Roger."

"At my command, turn to one-zero-two. Ready, execute."

"Coming left to one-zero-two."

"Maintain heading; no further acknowledgment is necessary unless an emergency arises.

"Begin five-hundred-foot-per-minute descent, now."

Throttling back, Bivens started his descent. Within seconds, he was down into the cloud, staring at the cottony white snow that drifted by his windshield.

For Ellie, it was a very disconcerting feeling. The airplane was moving through space at well over ninety miles per hour, yet she couldn't see more than a few feet ahead. She looked back at the cylinder-head temperature gauges, then gasped.

"This one is in the red!" she said.

"Thanks," Bivens said, enriching the fuel mixture on number two.

"Come left, two degrees," Dooley's voice said.

Bivens made the correction.

"You are too high," Dooley said.

Bivens dropped the nose slightly.

Suddenly the fire-warning bell started ringing and, looking out the right window, Bivens could see heavy black smoke streaming back from the engine cowl as little fingers of flame licked around it.

"We're on fire!" Ellie said. Her voice was raised in alarm, but she didn't scream.

"Yeah," Bivens said. "I see that."

He pulled the throttle and mixture controls all the way back on number two, then shut off the fuel feed. The flames continued to lick back across the cowl. The spinning propeller slowed, then as Bivens feathered it, the spinning stopped altogether, the blades hanging motionless and knife-edge into the wind.

"Now, hit the foam!" Bivens ordered.

"What?"

"That red button there. Push it in!" Bivens said, pointing to the fire extinguisher button.

Ellie hit the button as directed, and a heavy white foam flooded the engine, then oozed out across the top of the nacelle. The licking flames and billowing smoke stopped, but the scorching effect of the fire could be clearly seen.

"Do you see any more fire?" Bivens asked.

"No," Ellie said.

"I'd better let Kotzebue know," Bivens said. Taking down the microphone, he called in. "Dooley, I've just had an engine fire up here."

"Do you have it under control?" There was absolutely no increase in the pitch of Dooley's voice, as it assumed the professional calm of a controller who had dealt with hundreds of emergencies over the years.

"Yes, the fire is out," Bivens replied. "But I had to shut the engine down."

"I'll get the crash equipment out for you."

"Thanks. Under the circumstances, I would not like to execute a missed approach."

"I'll get you down the first time, Bob, I promise," Dooley replied. "You are looking good now, you are on course, on glide path."

Dooley's soundings continued with monotonous regularity as, on only one engine now, they descended through the blowing snow.

"Your altitude is fifteen hundred feet. You are six miles from the end of the runway.

"Please check landing gear down."

Bivens grabbed the lever with the little wheel-shaped handle and shoved it down. He looked at the gear indicator until the windows were in the green.

"Gear down and locked," he reported.

"Your altitude is five hundred feet. You are two miles from the end of the runway," Dooley said. "You are on course, on glide path."

"Two hundred fifty feet, one and one-half mile from end of runway. You are below glide path."

Bivens added a touch of throttle and the remaining engine responded with a slight increase in sound as the descent flattened a little.

"Two hundred fifty feet, one mile from end of runway. You are slightly left of course."

Bivens pressed down with his right foot and just touched right aileron.

"Two hundred feet, one-half mile from end of runway. On course, on glide path."

Bivens put the flaps down full.

"One hundred feet, one-quarter mile from end of runway. Bob, this is as far as I can get you with what I've got rigged up. You're going to have to take over now and land visually."

"Land visually?" Bivens said. "I can't see diddly squat!"

"We've got the high-intensity edge lights on. Look for them."

Bivens pulled the throttle all the way back, and the engine popped and backfired in protest. The plane continued to settle down through the white. Then, ahead of them, Ellie saw the twinkling of runway lights.

"The light!" she called, pointing through the windshield.

"Yeah, I see."

Bivens flattened out just above the runway, let the airplane glide for a long moment, then, as he began dissipating airspeed and altitude, gradually came back on the yoke until, finally, the tires kissed the runway. The landing was so smooth that it was difficult to determine exactly when they stopped flying and started rolling.

"Look out!" Ellie called.

A Jeep had appeared in front of them, with a large orange-and-white-checkered board mounted on the back. The white sign with black lettering read: FOLLOW ME.

"Holy Cow!" Bivens said. He put on the toe brakes, but the airplane continued to slide forward and he had to let up on them to keep from ground looping. Fortunately, the Jeep accelerated just enough to keep from being run over. "Where did he come from?"

"I don't know. He just suddenly appeared," Ellie said.

"Good job pointing him out," Bivens said. "Coming through this soup on one engine, then crashing into a Jeep on the ground—that wouldn't have been a happy ending. No, sir, that wouldn't have been a happy ending at all."

Turning off the active, the Jeep led them past two crash and rescue vehicles which were waiting in place to deal with any emergency. They left the taxiway and reached the parking apron, where a man stood holding up a couple of wand lights high over his head. Using the lights, he guided the plane into position, then made a cutting motion across his neck.

With the engine silent, the only sound to be heard was the hum of descending gyros as Bivens began turning off switches and shutting valves.

Looking over at Ellie, Bivens saw that she had a death grip on the sides of her seat. He smiled.

"You can let go of the seat now," he said. "We're here."

"I can't let go," Ellie said in a tight voice.

"Well, you're either going to have to let go or buy it. Which will it be?" Bivens teased.

Gradually, Ellie released her grip on the seat, then she held her hands up in front of her and looked at them. "Ah," she said, though it was more of an audible sigh than a word. "We made it."

"Yeah," Bivens replied, unbuckling his belt. "Feels good, doesn't it?"

～ Fifteen ～

"What do you mean, you need to find a hotel room?" Viki Bollinger, an attractive brunette, asked over the dinner table. "Why, you'll do no such thing. We have a spare room. You'll stay with us. Kevin has told me all about you, and any friend of Kevin's is a friend of mine."

"I wouldn't want to put you out any," Ellie said.

"Nonsense, you won't be putting us out," Kevin said. "Besides, it will give us an opportunity to talk, not only to catch each other up, but to plan our strategy for the appeal tomorrow."

"I'm just amazed that the judge agreed to hear it so quickly. I've always heard of appeals being dragged out for months."

"Well, normally, that is the case. But the judge bought the argument that this is time-sensitive because of Christmas. And, also, it is pretty simple," Kevin said. "The district judge didn't issue a finding, only a temporary injunction. So, if we can make our case, it won't be hard for him to set that aside."

"How do you feel about it?" Ellie asked.

"What do you mean?"

"If you were the appellate judge, what would your decision be?"

"At this point, I would tend to support Judge Fugate's position," Kevin said.

"Really?" Ellie said, disappointment evident in her tone.

"I believe strongly in the separation of church and state."

"Oh. Well, then, what chance do we have if my own lawyer is against me?"

At that moment a baby cried from a back room and, smiling, Viki stood. "I'd better go see to him."

"Bring him in here, hon," Kevin said. "I want to show him off to Ellie."

"All right, soon as I make sure he's fit to come in," Viki said.

"Ellie, I'm not against you," Kevin said, as Viki left the room. "You asked me what my opinion would be and I told you that, at this point, it would be to support Judge Fugate's decision. Give me something to work with. Why do you hold it in the school gym, when every court decision for the last several years has gone against that?"

"Because the gym is the only place large enough for it."

Kevin shook his head. "Not good enough," he said.

"Do you know anything about Point Hope?" Ellie asked.

"I looked it up on the map when you went there," Kevin said. "I know it's a whaling village."

"Yes. It is also a village with a very old history and a very rich culture. No other village in Alaska has a Christmas Festival quite like this. Certainly no other city in America. It dates back several hundred years."

Kevin laughed. "Are you saying they were celebrating Christmas in Alaska even before the American continent was settled?"

"No. Christmas has only been celebrated in Point Hope for just a little over a hundred years. But over that time, the Christmas Festival has become so intermixed with the ancient festivals that it is very difficult to see where one starts and the other leaves off."

Viki returned with the baby. Then, and for the next several minutes, Ellie was entertained by the antics, not only of the child but of his parents.

"Let me sleep on it," Kevin said. "I'll have a case to present to the judge tomorrow."

Ellie smiled at him. "I know you will, Kevin," she said. "When this came up, I didn't hesitate a second to call you. I have all the confidence in the world that you will be able to help us."

The sign, in raised brass letters, read: UNITED STATES COURT OF APPEALS FOR THE NINTH CIRCUIT.

Inside, a colonnade ran the entire length of the building, flanked on one side by the front of the building itself, and on the other by high, arching windows. Ornate chandeliers hung from the ceiling at intervals of approximately fifty feet.

Ellie sat on a bench in the colonnade, so overwhelmed by the power and sweep of the building that she began to have second thoughts about her mission. What was she doing here, anyway? What made her think that an institution this imposing, powerful, and important would have the time, or even the inclination, to deal with something as insignificant as the Point Hope Christmas Festival?

People walked up and down the colonnade, their footfalls making hollow pops against the marble floor. From the farthest end of the foyer a door slammed, sending its report echoing up and down the long hallway.

Turning in her seat, Ellie looked through the window out onto the street at the steady flow of traffic. She remembered how much she had hated the Dallas traffic, especially on LBJ; but now, she found something familiar, warm, and comforting about seeing a stream of cars on the road. Very few of the children in her class had ever seen anything like this.

"Ellie," Kevin called. When she didn't respond, he called a second time. "Ellie, are you ready?"

Looking around, Ellie saw that Kevin had just stepped out of one of the doors.

He motioned to her. "Come on. We don't have a lot of time. Judge Heckemeyer has agreed to hear our petition at ten. That's just five minutes from now."

"I'm on my way."

Ellie walked quickly to catch up with Kevin, then followed him through one of the doors.

"What courtroom will we be using?" she asked.

Kevin chuckled. "No courtroom," he answered. "We'll do this in the judge's chambers."

"You mean his office?"

"Yes. Here it is," he said.

The name on the frosted-glass door identified it as the office of Anthony J. Heckemeyer, Associate Justice. Kevin held the door open, then followed Ellie into the little outer office where a middle-aged woman looked up from her desk.

"Just a moment, Mr. Bollinger," she said, smiling pleasantly. "I'll tell the judge you are here."

A moment later, Kevin and Ellie stepped into Judge Heckemeyer's office. Judge Heckemeyer was a rather rotund man, with a round, puffy face, a pug nose, and a bald head.

He pointed to a leather couch, flanked on either end by leather chairs. "Let's sit over there, shall we? I think we will be more comfortable."

"Thank you, Your Honor," Kevin said. Kevin and Ellie sat on the sofa; the judge took one of the chairs. A manila folder was on a table beside him, and the judge picked it up and looked at it for a moment.

"I hope you have a compelling argument, Mr. Bollinger," he said, as he closed the folder and put it back down. "As you know, the precedence of separating church from state is well established and has upheld through many court cases and appeals. I'm going to have to hear something very strong from you to set this aside."

"Your Honor, the festival in Point Hope is much more than a Christmas Festival," Kevin began. "It is a festival that has been celebrated—not for hundreds but for thousands of years. Point Hope is the oldest continuously occupied community in the Western Hemisphere, and what this order will do is deprive Point Hope of its heritage."

"How does the fact that Point Hope is the oldest settled community have anything to do with celebrating Christmas? Obviously, before the arrival of Western culture, they were not celebrating Christmas."

"No, they weren't, Your Honor, but they were celebrating in essentially the same way. You see, it's all tied in with the whale celebration, and Christmas just added something to it, that's all."

"Then, if they took Christmas out, and just had the whale celebration, there would be no impact whatever on their heritage," Judge Heckemeyer said. "So, why don't you just call it a whale celebration that happens to occur around Christmas?"

"Your Honor, the Episcopal Church has had a presence there since 1890," Kevin said. "That means that for five generations, Christmas *has* been a part of their heritage. If you take Christmas away from them now, it will have a negative impact on everyone there. Not just about everyone, you understand, but everyone."

"Obviously not," Judge Heckemeyer said. He picked up the file. "A Mr. Galen Scobey has made the complaint that having the Christmas celebration in the school gym denotes official sanction of a particular religious belief and would impose that belief on his son."

"He is a visitor, Your Honor, with no vested interest in Point Hope or its culture. He arrived only a few weeks ago, and he will be leaving shortly after this Christmas. So in essence what you have is an interloper who appears only long enough to have a disruptive effect on the rest of the community."

Judge Heckemeyer put the file down, then looked at Ellie. "Where do you figure in this, Miss Springer? Are you a permanent resident there?"

"I've been there for three years," Ellie replied. "I'm a schoolteacher."

"Then you should understand, even if they don't, that the government cannot take part in advancing a particular faith."

"Judge, have you ever sat white-knuckled in a small airplane, unable to see ten feet in front of you, all your instruments out, depending upon someone on the ground to talk you down?"

Judge Heckemeyer shook his head. "What? No, I can't say that I have," he replied, somewhat confused by the question.

"Well, I have. Two days ago, a pilot, who is also a *nalokme*," Ellie said, but the judge interrupted her.

"A what?"

"A *nalokme*. It means someone who is not a native. Mr. Bob Bivens, who is not a native, put his life at risk to fly me out of Point Hope so I could catch a plane to come here. We never should have taken off, and it was a miracle that we weren't killed trying to land in the middle of a whiteout. Where do I figure in this? I figured that it was well worth the risk to save Christmas for those people. And I would do it again."

"I see," Judge Heckemeyer said. He drummed his fingers on the arm of the chair and looked at Ellie for a long moment. "Miss Springer, I can't tell you how much I admire you for risking your life for a cause in which you believe so deeply. But I believe in something as well. I believe in the oath of office I took to support and defend the Constitution of the United States. And, if I overturn Judge Fugate's order . . . if I let the religious belief of some hold sway over the religious belief of others, then I will be going against everything I stand for."

"Judge, what about one man's faith holding sway over the religious belief of many?" Kevin asked.

Judge Heckemeyer cocked his head. "I'm not sure where you are going with this?"

"Do you believe in God?"

"I don't think my personal belief is relevant in this case," Judge Heckemeyer said. "So, I'm not going to answer that."

"All right, you will agree with this, though, won't you, that there are only two possibilities for the universe? Order or chaos?"

"I suppose."

"If it is chaos, then God probably does not exist. But if it is order, then, while that in itself is not evidence of the existence of God, many believe there must be some direction to that order. What we are left with now are two possibilities. God does exist. God does not exist. Can either case be proven?"

"No, of course not," Judge Heckemeyer replied.

"Then, since the existence of God cannot be proven, those who believe that there is no God must do so by faith. Can faith be supported by the government?"

"No, it cannot."

Ellie looked at Kevin, confused and disturbed by the direction he was going. After all, last night he had told her that he, too, believed in separation of church and state.

"Well, since it cannot be proven that God does not exist, atheism is a faith. In this case, the faith that there is no God."

"Get to the point, Mr. Bollinger," Judge Heckemeyer said.

"My point is this, Your Honor. If faith in God cannot be supported by the government, then neither should faith in atheism be supported by the government. And if that is the case, why should the position of the atheist, whose religion is to see to it that no one else can practice their faith, be supported by the government?"

"But the government isn't supporting a faith, it is supporting a lack of faith," Judge Heckemeyer said.

Kevin shook his head. "Your Honor, as there is no perfect vacuum, there is no such thing as a lack of faith. It all comes down to one of two things. Faith that God exists, or faith that God does not exist.

"If the government allows the faith of the non-believer to hold sway over the faith of the believer, then that is not only a violation of the separation of church and state; it goes beyond that. It is a denial of the freedom of religion.

"In the final analysis, Your Honor, the non-believer always has the option of not attending the Christmas Festival. But, if you do not allow the festival, the believers will have no option at all."

"What about the agnostic who doesn't know which premise to accept?" Judge Heckemeyer asked. "Where does he fit in this equation?"

"The agnostic has taken himself completely out of the equation," Kevin replied. "He neither believes nor disbelieves. Consequently, whichever position the government supports—whether it be for the atheist or the believer—the agnostic is neither challenged nor sustained."

Judge Heckemeyer stroked his chin as he studied Kevin for a long moment. Then he chuckled.

"That is about the most convoluted argument I have ever heard," he said.

Ellie felt her heart sink.

"So convoluted that I can actually see its logic," Heckemeyer continued.

Now Ellie felt a quick surge of hope.

"This is what I'm going to do. I'm going to overrule Judge Fugate's writ *pro tempore*."

"Oh, thank you, Your Honor!" Ellie cried.

Heckemeyer held up his hand. "This will allow the people of Point Hope to hold their celebration this year," he said. "But if Mr. Scobey re-files his lawsuit, I'm not sure your argument is persuasive enough to prevent a permanent ban."

"I don't think Galen Scobey will have an interest in stopping any future Christmas celebrations," Ellie said.

Judge Heckemeyer stood, a signal to Ellie and Kevin to stand as well.

"You can consider the order lifted, as of now," Heckemeyer said. "I will get all the paperwork and electronic notification taken care of."

"What should I do now?" Ellie asked.

Heckemeyer smiled broadly. "Just have a Merry Christmas," he said.

~ Sixteen ~

Dear Ellie:

I'm sure I have forfeited the right to call you Ellie and if so I apologize. I would like to try and explain why I did what I did. Perhaps, if you understood my motivation, you would not judge me so . . .

Galen paused in the middle of the sentence, then wadded the letter up and tossed it into the trash can. He was probably foolish to even think about writing to her. He was sure she wouldn't bother to read it, and she had every right not to.

Still, he felt some need to reach out to her, if for no other reason than the fact that she was Nels's teacher.

Dear Miss Springer:
Talk of your exploits is all over the village, and rightly so as . . .

No, that wouldn't do it, either. Once more, Galen wadded up the paper and tossed it into the trash can beside his writing table. Getting out another sheet of paper, he stared at it a long time before he began his third effort.

Dear Miss Springer:

You are the most noble, sincere, and courageous person I have ever met. It is very sobering to think that you could have been killed because I am too weak to face the emotional trauma of Christmas.

I offer you my most sincere apologies with the full understanding that you have every right not to accept them.

Sincerely,
Galen Scobey

Satisfied with this one, Galen put it in an envelope and mailed it to Ellie.

The next afternoon, Galen was sitting at the table in his room, looking at the latest test results, when there was a knock on the door.

It was Molly.

"Ellie is in the parlor," Molly said coolly.

Molly, who had been almost motherly to Galen before, was now very distant since he had tried to stop the Christmas Festival.

"Do you know what she wants?" Galen asked.

"She wants to see you. I have no idea why she wants to see you, but she does."

"Thank you."

Galen followed Molly down the hall to the front of the house. Ellie was standing there, looking out through the front door.

The news of Ellie's trip to San Francisco had spread all through the village. Her stature with the villagers had reached heroic level, first because of the hazardous flight, and then because she managed to get the celebration restored.

When Galen heard the details of her flight to Kotzebue, how she could've been killed, he blamed himself. He had not spoken to her since her return because he didn't think he could face her.

"Miss Springer?" he said.

When Ellie turned to face him, he was glad to see that her face wasn't twisted with anger or, worse, hate.

"Thank you for the letter, Galen," she said. "It was very nice of you."

"I, uh, should've come seen you in person," he said. "The fact that you've come to me shows which of us has the greater courage. Of course, I don't think the issue was ever really in doubt."

"You're being too hard on yourself."

"I've just joined the crowd," Galen said. "Everyone is hard on me now. And I can't blame them."

"Would you like to take a walk?"

Galen laughed.

"What is it?"

"Only in Point Hope, Alaska, would taking a walk in a minus-five-degree temperature be considered a serious option."

"If you're dressed warmly enough, it's not so bad," Ellie said. "Get dressed. I'll wait."

One of the more unusual aspects of the snow up here, Galen noticed, was that you didn't sink down into it as you walked. Because of the cold temperature, soon after any snowfall it crusted over as hard as ice. They were wearing their mukluks as they walked, but he could just as easily have been wearing street shoes, though of course it was much too cold for that.

Amazingly, though, their winter gear warded off the extreme cold, and as they walked it was no more uncomfortable than would have been a brisk, fall day with a sweater somewhere down in the lower forty-eight.

"Nels told me about his mother dying during the Christmas season," Ellie said.

"Yes."

"It is understandable, then, why Christmas is so hard for you."

"No," Galen said. "It's not understandable. I can't even understand it myself."

They walked on in silence for a moment longer, then Galen spoke again.

"Others grieve and get over it. I have relished it. I wear it as I wear this parka, only instead of keeping out the cold, I keep out life."

"I should've been more sensitive to it," Ellie said. "I shouldn't have pushed you to let Nels be in the play."

"I want him to be in the play," Galen said. "That is, if you still have a place for him."

"Yes, of course I do."

"Good. I want him to be in the play, and to participate fully in all the activities. I had no right to impose my problems on him."

"Have you told him that?"

"Yes. I told him as soon as I heard that the court order had been set aside."

"I'm sure he's very pleased that the two of you will be participating."

"No, you misunderstood. Not the two of us," Galen said. "Just Nels."

"Oh?"

"I'm not quite ready to make that step yet."

"Well, I won't try to talk you into changing your mind," Ellie said. "I'm just glad that you are going to allow Nels to take part."

"Why did you do it?" Galen asked. "Why did you risk your life to get the judge's order turned around?"

Ellie giggled. "Believe me, Galen, if someone had told me what kind of flight we were going to have, I wouldn't have done it."

"No . . . I think you would have done it no matter what the risk."

"Maybe." Ellie was quiet for a moment. "Have you ever watched *Star Trek*?"

"*Star Trek*? Well, yes, who hasn't?"

"The Prime Directive," Ellie said.

"The Prime Directive," Galen repeated. It was obvious he had no idea what she was talking about.

"Don't you remember the Prime Directive? To do nothing that would alter another civilization. I look on the people of Point Hope almost as another civilization—self-contained, unique, proud. I did not want to be a party, even indirectly, in denying them something that is so important to them."

"I'm glad you kept me from making a terrible mistake," Galen said.

"So, changing the subject, how goes the search for oil?"

Galen smiled. "Looks like you're about to win on that one, too," he said. "I haven't seen anything that would make me recommend further exploration. Though there is one area I want to look at again."

"I'm sorry," Ellie said.

"Sorry? I thought you wanted a negative report."

"I'm not sorry about that," Ellie said. "I'm glad there won't be a major impact on the village. But, on a personal level, I'm sorry that your visit up here wasn't productive."

"Well, fortunately, my salary doesn't depend upon my finding oil. All I have to do is look for it," Galen replied with a chuckle. "And I wouldn't say my visit up here has been completely non-productive. I learned a lot about myself. I don't like what I learned . . . but I did learn."

By now, they had made a big circle and were back at the Kowan-nas'. Ellie unplugged the heating element from her snowmobile, then climbed on.

"Ellie?"

Ellie looked up.

"Thank you."

Ellie nodded, then started the engine. Galen waited as she drove away, then he went back inside.

Molly had been watching through the window, and now she hurried to get back into her chair before Galen came in. She said nothing to him as he passed by on the way back to his room. Then, she picked up her paperback and started reading where she had left off. It was near the end of the book; the last major obstacle had been overcome, and it seemed headed for a happy ending.

Molly smiled.

When Ellie's class finished the Nativity play, the audience applauded appreciatively. After the children took their bows, parents, relatives, and friends hurried up to congratulate them.

Ellie saw Nels standing to one side, watching his classmates meeting with their families. She felt a wave of sympathy for him, and hurried over to talk to him.

"You read beautifully, Nels," Ellie said. "But, then, I knew you would."

"Thank you, Miss Springer," Nels replied. Then he smiled. "Or are you just telling me that because you think us *nalokmes* should stick together?"

Ellie laughed, then embraced Nels and kissed him on top of his head.

"*Nalokmes* unite," she said. "Are you ready for the games?"

"I'm more ready for the games than I am the food," Nels said. "What's that stuff they're eating?" He pointed to two young Eskimo children, a boy and a girl, who were obviously enjoying a treat they had taken from a big bowl at the end of one of the tables.

"You mean *mactac*?"

"That awful-looking, awful-smelling black stuff."

Ellie nodded. "Yes," she said. *"Mactac."*

"What *is* that?"

"It's whaleskin and blubber," Ellie said. "As you can see by the way those little children love it, it's quite a treat for the Eskimos. But I wouldn't recommend it as an appetizer you might enjoy. Come on over to the table; let's see what they've laid out for our feast."

Leading Nels to the table, she pointed out the food and named it for him. "*Koc*, well, that's just raw fish, so if you've ever eaten sushi, I guess it isn't all that bad. Raw whale, raw bearded seal, and caribou soup. But the greatest delicacy of all is whale flipper."

"Is it eaten raw too?"

"Yes."

"Yuk," Nels said. "Have you eaten all of that stuff?"

"Many times," Ellie replied. "As a schoolteacher, I'm sort of expected to."

"How do you do that?"

Ellie reached down into her pocket and pulled out a handful of crackers. "I learned the first year I was here to always carry crackers with me," she told him. "Most of the stuff they give you, I can manage to get down, if I eat a cracker with it. But, and here is the best secret of all, learn how to say no."

"Whoa! Now *that* doesn't look bad," Nels said, pointing to a plate of jiggly red and green.

"That's Jell-O," Ellie said. "They're big on Jell-O and Kool-Aid up here, probably because they're in powder form and easy to transport and store. Oh, and there's Eskimo ice cream."

"Ice cream? I like ice cream." Picking up a bowl and spoon, he started toward it.

"Nels," Ellie called. "Wait."

"Oh, you mean wait for dessert?"

Ellie laughed. "No. I mean, wait until I tell you what Eskimo ice cream is."

"What is it?"

"It's berries and meat, whipped up in shortening. It's a little like raw cookie dough, except you don't have any sugar, eggs, or chocolate chips."

"Isn't there anything in here to eat that's normal?" Nels asked in a pained voice.

"Oh yes. If you look further down you'll see scalloped potatoes, salads, rolls, baked beans, and roast caribou. And don't forget Mrs. Kowanna's pumpkin pies."

"Nels, you better hurry or all the good stuff will be gone," Rex Hale called as he passed by.

"You mean raw whalemeat?"

"Nah, there's plenty of that. I'm talking about the Rice Krispie treats."

Nels smiled broadly. "Rice Krispie treats? Why didn't you say so?"

He ran to the table, grabbed a handful of the little squares, then came back to stand near Ellie.

"Do you think there's any chance your father will change his mind and come to the celebration?" Ellie asked.

"No, ma'am," Nels said, as he took a bite of the treat. "But he said I could have a good time."

"I just wish he would come join us," Ellie said.

"He won't," Nels said. "He thinks everyone is still mad at him." He poked a dangling Rice Krispie treat into his mouth. "I think they are too."

~ Seventeen ~

"Yes!" Galen said triumphantly, as he saw the little orange tripod he and Amos had left out in the field the day before. He headed over toward it, then shut down the engine of his snowmobile.

"Who needs a guide when you've got GPS?" he said aloud.

Climbing off the machine, Galen walked back to the sled and began getting out the equipment he would need. He had already checked this area, and though the results weren't exactly positive, there were some interesting anomalies. Those variations from all the other tests were the only thing that was keeping him from submitting a negative report.

As he worked, he checked his watch and realized that he would not have everything done before dark. But the northern lights had been particularly brilliant for the last several nights. Last night they were so bright that he and Amos started back and drove for some distance before they realized they hadn't turned on the snowmobile lights.

"Ellie, let's hope your big old electric light bulb is just as bright tonight," he said.

He thought about Ellie, and all the trouble he had caused her. If he could go back and change things, he would not have attempted to stop the Christmas Festival. In fact, he almost went to the play today. He did want to see Nels perform. But he remembered the animosity everyone felt toward him and the "spell" Kingik had put on him.

Galen put his hand in his pocket and pulled out the little *tikituk* Kingik had thrown at him that day in the Native Store. It was intricately carved from whalebone, and Galen couldn't help but marvel at the time that went into carving it.

"Well, Tiki," he said. "I haven't figured out yet whether I should keep you as a souvenir or throw you away to break the spell. I'll say this for you. You're more interesting than a pet rock and less trouble than a pet dog."

Laughing at his own observation, Galen began setting up for the series of tests he would be performing.

"Here comes Santa Claus!" someone shouted, and everyone in the gym turned toward the front door to see the entrance.

"Ho, ho, ho!" Santa shouted, waving at the children who flocked toward him.

"That's Mr. Kowanna," Nels said.

"Yes, but don't give him away," Ellie told him.

Although Ahlook had predicted that Gus Kowanna was too mean to be Santa, he was the picture of joviality today, smiling and laughing at the children as he passed out gifts.

"It's time for the games. *Ungasiksikaq* on this side, *Qagmaktoq* on that," Gus Kowanna said, pointing to opposite ends of the court.

Quickly, the village divided into two groups, sitting on the floor on either side of the gym.

"What are *Ungasiksikaq* and *Qagmaktoq*?" Nels asked, struggling with the words.

"The village is divided into two groups according to whaling crews," Ellie explained. "In the old days, when the *Qagmaktoq* returned from a whale hunt, they would draw their boats up on the north beach, and the *Ungasiksikaq* would land their boats on the south beach. Now, they all use the north beach, but the *Qagmaktoq* point their boats toward the north and the *Ungasiksikaq* point their boats toward the south."

"Whoa. Do they ever get mad at each other?"

"Maybe in the old days," Ellie said. "A thousand years or so ago. But now, it's all social."

Isaac Ahlook stepped out from the *Ungasiksikaq* side, and walked to the middle of the gym floor. "Who will face me in the finger pull?" he challenged.

"I will," Mark Hale answered, and, to the supporting cheers of the *Qagmaktoq,* Hale went out to face Ahlook. The two men sat on the floor, looked at each other for a moment, then reached out and locked their fingers together.

Amidst the cheers and support of both sides, the men pulled against each other.

That was when the lights went out.

As Galen had predicted, the aurora borealis provided enough light so that, even when the sun set, he was able to continue his work. It wasn't an unusual experience for him; several times during his exploration he and Amos Hale had continued to work after sunset.

Galen had made four shots from four different locations. Normally, four would be enough, but he wanted to be very sure, so he decided to take one more. The results of tonight's operation would probably provide him with the information he needed to make a final decision.

He started moving the tripods around, putting them in a position that would give him a completely bracketed read of the subterranean layers—some of which might hold oil.

At first, he didn't really notice the decrease in light, but then it grew dark very quickly. Looking up toward the northern lights, he saw that they, and the stars, were blocked out by clouds. Then, holding out his arm, he saw little flecks of snow falling onto his parka.

Glad that he had only one more shot, he set it off, then gathered the printout roll, stuck it in his parka, and loaded the equipment onto the sled. It was getting darker. Much darker.

Galen twisted the key in the snowmobile ignition. The engine groaned, but barely turned over.

"No," he said aloud. "No, don't do this to me." He tried again. This time the engine didn't turn over at all.

"All right," he said to the machine. "Freeze up on me and see if I care. I'll leave you here and walk back."

Galen knew that he hadn't come all that far from Point Hope. Maybe five miles at the most. He could walk it back in about an hour.

Who was he kidding? Out here just moving was an effort, what with the cold and, now, the snow, which was increasing in intensity. Five miles under these conditions could take as much as two hours.

Well, two hours wasn't that big of a problem. He'd already been out here for more than two hours. And who's to say it would take him that long to get back, anyway? It was just a matter of getting his bearings, then starting out. Nothing to it.

He checked his GPS.

It wasn't working!

*   *   *

Back in the village the celebration continued, illuminated now by scores of lanterns.

"After all, our grandparents didn't have electricity for these festivals," Ahlook said.

Pointing to the very bright, commercial lanterns, Koonook said, "They didn't have gas lanterns either."

The games continued, and whoever won the contest remained in the middle of the floor, challenging all comers until he was defeated.

Ahlook was the undefeated finger-pull champion, but Henry Killigivuk, the school janitor, was the champion ear-puller. Even the children got into the games and Nels, because he was a particular friend of Rex Hale's, was declared an honorary member of the *Ungasiksikaq*.

"Come on!" Rex called. "It's the tug-of-war!"

All of the children, boys and girls, participated, and because their effort would add or detract points for their respective groups, they were cheered as enthusiastically as the adults were. To the congratulations of many, Nels's side, the *Ungasiksikaq*, won.

After the games, some of the men moved the volleyball poles into the middle of the court. Nels thought they were getting ready to have a volleyball game; but instead, they hung a curtain between the two poles, dividing the court into two halves.

"Come on," Rex said. "We're *Ungasiksikaq*. We're on this side."

"What's going to happen?"

"The *Qagmaktoq* are going to feed us," Rex said.

"They are going to *feed* us? Why?"

"Because we fed them last year," Rex explained.

"Miss Springer, which are you?" Nels asked.

Ellie laughed. "Well, I'm neither. Which means, I suppose, that I can be either."

"Then you come with us," Nels said. "You can be my parent."

Ellie started to protest that as a schoolteacher she shouldn't join either group, but the sincerity of Nels's request won her over.

"All right," she said. "I hereby declare myself a member of the *Ungasiksikaq*."

"Hooray!" Nels said.

"Boy, if we had a shooting contest, and Miss Springer was on our side, the *Ungasiksikaq* would win for sure," Rex said.

"Why? Is Miss Springer a good shot?"

"Are you kidding? She's the best shot in Alaska. Maybe the best shot anywhere!"

"Where do we eat?" Nels asked.

"Right here," Rex said.

"Where are the tables?"

Rex laughed. "You really are a *nalokme*, aren't you? There aren't any tables. We sit on the floor."

Galen had gotten his initial bearings by following the tracks made by the snowmobile. That at least started him in the right direction. But as the snow continued to fall, the trail was covered, so he could no longer use the tracks as his guide.

He comforted himself with the fact that, if he was going in the right direction, he couldn't get lost. Even if he missed the village, he was pretty sure he'd be able to tell when he reached the coast; then it was just a matter of turning one way or the other to get to the village. Of course, that all depended on whether he reached the coast north or south of the village. And if he hit the little finger of land that Point Hope was on, he should be able to find the village very easily.

To do that, he would have to keep himself walking in as straight a line as he could. But he knew that in the dark, without any kind of orientation, that would be very, very difficult. He could wind up so far off course that . . . Galen gasped. His survival kit! He'd left it back on the sled!

Should he go back and get it? How far back was it? It had to be two or three miles by now. Surely he was closer to the village than he was to his snowmobile. Besides, could he even find it if he went back? Heading for the coast was one thing, but trying to find a snowmobile and sled out in the middle of ten thousand square miles of frozen wasteland was something entirely different.

He had no choice. He would have to keep going.

"Oh, Lord," he said. "Don't let me die out here! What would happen to Nels with both his parents dead?"

Galen stopped and put his mitten up to his forehead. Was that a prayer? Had he just said a prayer? When was the last time he had prayed? He was sure he hadn't prayed since Julia died.

When he pulled his hand down, it broke off some of the frost from the ruff that encircled the parka hood. The situation was bad, and it was getting worse.

~ Eighteen ~

"Ellie, can I speak with you for a second?" Sam Keating asked. He had a worried expression on his face.

"Yes, of course," Ellie replied, wondering what this was about. Excusing herself, she set her plate down on the floor, got up, then followed Sam to the back of the room. There, she saw Amos Hale, Mark Hale, and Isaac Ahlook.

"Here she is," Sam said to the men.

"What is it? What's wrong?" Ellie asked.

"A storm has come up," Mark said.

"Yes, go on."

"Galen Scobey is out on the tundra," Amos said.

"What? No, he's over in his room," Ellie said. Then, when she saw the look on their faces, she added, almost plaintively, "Isn't he?"

Amos shook his head. "He said he had one more place that he wanted to run tests on. He wanted me to go with him, but I told him I would not go until after Christmas."

"So, what are you telling me? That he went alone?"

"Yes. He went alone."

"Do you think he's in trouble?"

Amos nodded. "I think maybe, yes. He does not know where he is. He uses a—" He made a motion with his hands, as if opening something, and Sam Keating supplied the word.

"GPS, the global positioning system."

"Yes. He uses that to find himself. But I think with this storm, he will not be able to get a signal."

"Oh," Ellie said, putting her hand to her mouth. She turned to look back toward Nels, who was bravely attempting to eat something Rex had given him. Rex and some of the others were laughing. "Oh, if anything happens to him, what will become of Nels?"

"I will talk to Luke," Amos said. "We will get a search party and go look for him."

"Do you think you can find him?"

"I know where he wanted to go," Amos said. "If he made it there, we can find him."

"Oh, thank you. Thank you very much."

The star appeared shortly after the snow stopped, but it was still so heavily overcast that the northern lights could not be seen. None of the other stars could be seen either, just this one single star, very low in the western horizon.

But, if there was only one star, he couldn't have asked for it to be in a better location than right straight ahead of him.

"All right, little star," Galen said aloud. He pointed to it. "If you'll just keep shining for me, like a good boy, then I'll be all right. I can use you to keep my bearings, and to keep from wandering off in circles."

Galen didn't normally talk to himself. But tonight wasn't normal. He needed to hear a human voice, even if it was his own.

As he looked at the star, he thought of the "Wandering Star" song from *Paint Your Wagon* that he and Nels would often sing, and he began to sing it now as he trudged on through the snow.

By the time he was finished with the song, it appeared to him that the star was even brighter.

It reminded him a little of the light over Reunion Tower in Dallas, and he remembered how Nels had told him that that light reminded him of his mother.

"Tell me, Julia, did you hang that star in the sky for me?" Galen asked. He chuckled. "You remember the Christmas tree star you bought? Well, I could sure use it about now."

The star continued to grow brighter, like a prayer answered.

Like a prayer answered. Was it a prayer answered?

"Lord? Did you let Julia put that star there for me?" Galen asked.

Galen thought of the Three Wise Men who had followed a star two thousand years ago, to pay their respects to the newly born Christ Child.

"Julia, I'm sorry," he said. "I know how much you loved Christmas. All these years, I should have been celebrating it as a memorial to you. Instead, I let my grief drive me away. But I'll not do so again. From now on, Nels and I will celebrate Christmas with the best of them. I promise you that."

By now, word that Galen was somewhere out on the tundra had spread throughout the gym, and all conversation turned in that direction. Nels, hearing the news, was frightened, but trying hard not to let his fear overcome him. Ellie stood near him with her arm around him.

"He'll be all right, Miss Springer," Nels said in a small voice. "He'll be all right."

"Yes, of course he will," Ellie answered. "The men of the village will find him."

As Ellie listened in on some of the conversations, she was surprised but very pleased to hear that everyone was genuinely concerned for Galen's safety, and that no one wished him harm.

"It looks like Mr. Scobey managed to take the Christmas celebration from us after all," Sunshine Komack said.

"Sunshine! What a terrible thing to say!" Ellie scolded.

"I want nothing to happen to him," Sunshine said quickly. "I just meant that, with the search party looking for him, the feast will have to stop."

"Would everyone who is going on the search please gather at the front door?" Koonook called. "We'll be leaving in a few minutes."

Ellie looked toward the front door and saw dozens of men standing there, dressed now not in their ceremonial clothes but in the down parkas and pants, mukluks, mittens, and hoods they would need to protect them from the weather during their trek.

Galen wasn't quite sure when he realized that the light he was following wasn't a star after all. Some of the symbolism was lost when he discovered that. But what he lost in symbolism was more than made up for by the happy realization that, if it was a light, it must be coming from the village. And, if it was coming from the village, then all he had to do was follow it to take him home.

He continued to trek through the snow, buoyed now by the light that continued to shine, unblinkingly, before him.

Finally, Galen reached the edge of the village where he saw, with some surprise, that the entire village was in darkness, except for the light he had been following. And that light was shining brilliantly from the top of the school gymnasium, so bright that it lit up the entire east end of the village. This, he knew, was the Star of Bethlehem that the village had paid a thousand dollars for. It was one of the decorations that had been put up by the villagers.

Galen remembered thinking what a waste of money that was when he heard how much the village council paid for it. Now, he thought there had never been money better spent.

As Galen stared at the light attached to the top of the gym, he felt an overwhelming sense of gratitude, and an awareness of God's presence. It was a feeling he had never experienced before, but that didn't diminish its validity. He knew exactly what it was, and he offered a prayer of thankfulness.

"Lord, thank you for leading me out of the wilderness. It has not escaped my notice that the Star of Bethlehem that guided the three Kings so long ago has now guided me home. And when I say home, I'm not just talking about my safe return to Point Hope."

Filled with "the light," and now safely within the limits of the village, Galen ran the remaining distance to the gym. He had lacked the courage, before, to see the villagers face to face, but he intended to do so now. And he planned to ask for everyone's forgiveness.

Also, if they would accept him, he intended to join in what was left of the celebration.

When Galen threw open the door, he was surprised to see that the gym was lighted by lanterns, rather than by the banks of overhead lights that made it bright enough to play basketball.

"Galen, thank God you're safe!" Ellie cried, running to him. Unashamedly, she embraced him, and he her. Then he reached down and picked up Nels.

The others came over to congratulate him as well, and he learned that a rescue party was being formed to go out onto the tundra and look for him.

"After what I did, you were still willing to risk your lives looking for me?" he said. "I can't tell you how moved I am by that."

"Yes, well, don't be too moved. To a *nalokme,* it would be risking your life. For us, it would just be an interruption in our festival," Mark Hale teased, and the others laughed.

"Yes, well, whether it would have been a risk for you or not, I thank you. And, as far as the celebration is concerned, I no longer wish to halt it. I have changed my whole attitude about Christmas. You might say I have seen the light." He laughed. "Literally," he said. "When my GPS quit working, I followed the light, and it led me here."

"You followed the light?" Koonook asked. "What light? What are you talking about?"

"The Star of Bethlehem," Galen said.

When the others looked at each other with an expression that told Galen they still didn't know what he was talking about, he explained.

"You know, that big light that you put on top of the gym? The one that you paid a thousand dollars for? I could see it from way out in the tundra when I couldn't see anything else. All I had to do was follow it."

The villagers continued to stare at him.

"By the way, does it have a dedicated generator? How did you turn it on when all the other lights are off?"

It suddenly dawned on Galen that, not only was nobody answering him, they were all staring at him open-mouthed.

"What is it?" he asked. "Why are you all looking at me like that?"

"Galen?" Ellie said.

"Yes?"

"Look over there."

Looking over on the stage, Galen saw the big light that the council had bought.

"The light was never put up," Ellie said. "They didn't get it up during the court injunction, and when the injunction was lifted, there wasn't time."

"What? No, that can't be right. There's a huge, very bright light sitting on top of the gym right now. Come on outside with me and I'll show you."

Everyone hurried outside to see the light Galen was talking about.

"It's right up—" Galen started to say, pointing to the top of the gym. He stopped in midsentence, and felt a tingling sensation on the back of his neck. There was nothing but darkness at the top of the gym. "I . . . I don't understand," he said quietly.

"It was Mom," Nels said. "God let her shine the light for you."

Once more, Galen put his arm around Nels and pulled him close.

"I think you are right," he said.

Suddenly all the lights in the village came back on, and there was a spontaneous cheer from everyone present. They rushed back inside to continue the celebration, and Galen went in with them.

As soon as everyone got back inside, six drummers moved to a position in front of the curtain that separated the two groups. The drums, made with whaleskin stretched tightly over willow hoops, were struck from below, and as they began the rhythmic percussion, there was a loud shout from the other side of the curtain.

"What's that?" Galen asked.

"That's the joy shout," Ellie explained. "It means the dancing is about to begin."

The first dancer appeared through the curtain, moved in front of the drummers, then made a slight jump to each side of the room.

"He is calling for his *kimmun*," Ellie told Galen.

"His *kimmun*?"

"His own song," Ellie said. "Almost everyone has their own song."

"How do they get their own song? Do they write them?"

"No, no, you can't write your own song. Someone else has to bestow that honor upon you. Most of the songs now are old ones, inherited from grandparents, great-grandparents, or more. Some of the songs are two or three hundred years old. It's a very rare honor for someone to have a new song."

As the dancing continued, Galen thought it was unlike anything he had ever seen. There was a lot of swaying back and forth, an occasional stomp of the feet and waving of hands. The hands were rarely ever empty, because the dancers held mittens or gloves, which they often waved at the audience.

After each dance, the dancer would distribute presents to someone, who would then be the next dancer.

"Ellie," Ahlook called. "Ellie, join us for the Hunting Dance."

"Oh, I don't know . . . ," Ellie started.

"Come, you must," Ahlook said.

As Ellie moved toward the curtain, she saw, in addition to Isaac Ahlook, Luke Koonook, Mark Hale, and Percy Tokomik. The entire hunting party was up for this dance.

The drums began beating. Luke Koonook stepped out front. He held up his hands and the drums stopped.

"And now, ladies and gentlemen, Percy Tokomik is going to sing the *kimmun* of Ellie Springer."

"What do you mean? I don't have a *kimmun*."

"You do now," Koonook said. "We wrote it for you. All of us," he said, waving at the others who had been part of the hunting party.

"I will sing it in English so that you can understand," Tokomik said.

Once more, the drums began to beat.

> *The ice pack came*
> *No more ships*
> *No meat, the village was hungry*

The caribou visited other lands
And we had to go find them.
A good hunter was needed, so
The one who is the best shot in the village
Was selected.
Ellie Springer killed the first caribou
And when the storm came she was brave.
Now the village is not hungry because
Ellie Springer is a good shot.

Ellie danced with the others as well as she could during the singing of her *kimmun,* and when the song was concluded, she left the dance floor amidst laughter and applause.

"Now, forever, you are one of us," Koonook said. "One hundred years from now, people will be singing your *kimmun.*"

"Luke, I cannot tell you how honored I am," Ellie said, her eyes brimming with tears.

When Ellie left the floor, Galen met her with a cup of coffee.

"Thanks," Ellie said. "I'll bet this tastes good to you after being out in the storm."

Galen chuckled as he tasted the coffee. "Uhmm," he said. "It would take a storm to make this stuff taste good."

Ellie laughed, put her hand on his chest, then leaned into him. Looking over Ellie's shoulder, Galen saw Molly Kowanna. Molly held up her paperback novel, pointed to it, then smiled broadly and nodded.